Good Connections is the .... difference. Gone are th........ and Duponts. Gone an........ never quite alphabeti........ reason for it).

At last, Dai Lintone, ..., has come up with a manageable selection of the globe's most useful, most interesting and most unusual telephone numbers.

Try dialling . . .

Lutoslawski, Witold   **Warsaw 392390**
Federação Portuguesa de Futebol   **Lisbon 328207**
Albanian Orthodox Diocese of America   **Jamaica Plains 5240477**
Fire Brigade (Buenos Aires)   **382222**
Kaohsiung International Wig Corporation
   Kaohsiung 220740
New Zealand Sunday School Union Book Shop
   Auckland 774059
Menuhin, Yehudi   **New York 2976900**
Penthouse Bar   **Singapore 371666**
Keaton, Diane   **Los Angeles 2746024**
Kalamazzoo College   **Kalamazzoo 3838497**
Simenon, Georges   **Lausanne 333979**
Gobbi, Tito   **Rome 990996**
OPEC   **Vienna 639780**
Sepahsalor Mosque Library   **Tehran 363738**
Sony   **Tokyo 4482111**

DAI LINTONE

Good Connections

PANTHER
Granada Publishing

Panther Books
Granada Publishing Ltd
8 Grafton Street, London W1X 3LA

First published by Panther Books 1983
Reprinted 1983

ISBN 0-586-05793-5

Printed and bound in Great Britain by
Collins, Glasgow

Set in Baskerville

CONTENTS

SAMARITANS?

INTRODUCTION

In March 1876 a laboratory assistant in Boston, Massachusetts, had a phone call from his boss, the Professor of Vocal Physiology. 'Mr Watson, come here, I want you,' the voice said; which may not seem very remarkable, except that these were the first words transmitted by telephone; the voice was that of Alexander Graham Bell and the world was never quite the same again.

'It talks!' exclaimed Emperor Pedro II of Brazil, encountering a telephone at its first public demonstration, and promptly dropping it on the floor, establishing a precedent that has been faithfully followed at times of stress throughout the world during the last hundred years.

By the time the telephone celebrated its centenary, 210,715 million calls were being made in one year, in America alone. (That is 979 calls per person, or 2.67 calls per person per day.)

Absolute privacy and freedom from interruption had been virtually annihilated by Bell's invention. What was Mr Watson doing in the next room? Perhaps he had no wish to be disturbed at all. But after that first fateful call neither he nor most of mankind had very much choice in the matter.

Within twenty-five years of Emperor Pedro's first gesture of defiance, one person in fifty in America had a telephone. One hundred years later, the ratio had risen to 718 telephones to 1,000 people and in certain areas, like Beverly Hills, the figures were as high as 1,600 telephones per 1,000 people.

Happy are the people of Pitcairn Island with their modest total of twenty-eight phones. Happy too are the people of Zaire who can boast having fewer than one telephone to every thousand people. For Bell's brainchild has brought

1

with it more than the facility of instant communication. Apart from the greatly eased intrusion of the mother-in-law and the creditor, it has brought frustrations that Bell could never have imagined.

While it may be possible to dial the other side of the world, it is equally likely that an urgent call to the local plumber or electricity board will be met by a recorded message and a machine to collect our outbursts of annoyance and despair.

The telephone may provide utilitarian convenience, but the last thing it offers is fun – that is until *Good Connections* came along . . .

Good Connections does for each of us what the Iranian Revolution did for Ayatollah Khomeini and what *E.T.* did for other galactic life-forms. It puts the world at your feet. Equipped with this unique telephone directory (and a phone of course) the entire globe becomes your plaything.

Have you ever wanted to put the world to rights? Look up Ronald Reagan under *Presidents* and give him a call on Washington DC 4562573. For good measure give Mr Andropov a call on Moscow 2062511 to get a balanced view of the latest global crisis. Select a strike force from the list under *Air Supremacy* and turn yourself into a super power overnight. On the other hand, a call to Colt Firearms on Hartford 2788550 will provide an impressive range of weapons to enable you to do the job yourself and at a fraction of the cost.

Have you ever been infuriated by the poor service at the local garage? Find out the head office and go straight to the man at the top (they're listed under *Motor Show*).

Have you ever felt at a loose end in America? Book yourself in at Bottoms Up (under *Rendez-vous*) on Atlanta 8751043, and if that fails try Fantasy Escorts East on Newark 6225560 and your problems will be solved.

Perhaps your problems are more than a passing phase? Worried by original sin? Call Soul Talk on Sydney 7476311 for spiritual reassurance about the after-life. Worried by life itself? Try Euthanasia Education Council on New York 2466962 (both under *Problem Solvers*).

Do you want to improve your golf drive? Call Lee Trevino on El Paso 5893466 for a little expert tuition.

Do you want to know what Dame Fate has in store for you? Call your star sign (under *Future Perfect?*) on New York 9365050/6262.

Do you want the best in Dialectical Materialist education for your children? Call Karl Marx University of Economic Sciences (under *College Connections*) on Budapest 286850.

Plumbers' telephone numbers you won't find in *Good Connections* but you *will* find thousands of invaluable numbers of a different sort. Whether you are after the telephone number of:

EDWARD KENNEDY
   Washington DC 2244543,
or QUEEN ELIZABETH II
   London 9304832,
whether you are looking for entertainment
at THE LOBSTER POT, NAIROBI
   Nairobi 20491,
at THE PARIS RITZ
   Paris 2603830,
at THE BAKU NIGHTSPOT
   Moscow 998094,
or for the luggage you lost
at MADRAS CENTRAL RAILWAY STATION
   Madras 38797,
whether you want to speak to
the HEAD OF NASA
   Houston 4830123,
the HEAD OF BOSS
   Johannesburg 8364551,
the HEAD OF THE CIA
   Washington DC 35111000,
or to one of the ETON COLLEGE BEAGLES
   Slough 24968,
whether you want to know what the weather is like
in BOMBAY
   Bombay 211654,
or how to get a Guinness on Sunday morning
in DUBLIN
   Dublin 756701 - this is the book for you.

Do you want to know what's going on everywhere, every
hour and every minute of the day? Do you want to have a
finger in every pie and an answer to every question? Do you
want to be put in touch with the world's most exciting and
influential people and places? Do you want, in short, to have
a hot line to the world? If you do, read on . . .

ACCIDENTS WILL HAPPEN
50 first-aid numbers to keep you going from Addis Ababa to Zurich

What happens when you get rammed by a rickshaw in Bangkok, jostled by a junk in Hong Kong or bruised by a bandito in Bogota? Probably nothing at all, unless you have the wherewithal to call for help yourself. This is how you do it. Dial:

Addis Ababa 01
Amsterdam 355555 or 782233
Athens 106 or 5255555
Auckland 111
Bangkok 13
Barcelona 2887274
Belgrade 94 or 97
Berlin 112
Bogota 453333
Brussels 900
Buenos Aires 344001
Chicago 0
Copenhagen 000 or 0041
Dublin 999
Frankfurt 112
Geneva 117
Glasgow 999
Helsinki 0066
Hong Kong 5761111 or 3855555
Istanbul 493000

Johannesburg 354141 or 7241121
Karachi 73259 or 70600
Kuala Lumpur 0
Lisbon 115 or 665342
London 999
Los Angeles 0
Madrid 2616199
Manila 596061 or 471081
Melbourne 000
Milan 3189955 or 7733
Montreal 8711112 or 9351101
Moscow 03
Munich 112
Nairobi 999
Nassau 22221
New York 0
Oslo 201090
Paris 17
Rio de Janeiro 2321234
Rome 555666

San Juan **7690710**	Tokyo **119**
Singapore **999**	Vancouver **8725151**
Stockholm **90000**	Vienna **144**
Sydney **000**	Washington DC **0**
Tel Aviv **101**	Zurich **117**

ACE OF CLUBS
a clubman's vade mecum

'Please accept my resignation,' Groucho Marx telegraphed one club secretary. 'I don't want to belong to any club that will accept me as a member.' 'It is easier for a man to be loyal to his club than to his planet,' wrote E. B. White in the *New Yorker*, 'the by-laws are shorter, and he is personally acquainted with the other members.' These are just two views of club life. For a closer look at that world within the world, why not try some of these when you're next in the neighbourhood.

Agra Club	**Agra 74084**
Alwiyah Club	**Baghdad 95115**
Arts Club	**Chicago 7873997**

Automobile Club of Southern California	**Los Angeles 7464380**
Avadh Gymnkhana Club	**Lucknow 23966**
British Club	**Bahrain 8245**
Cannes Country Club	**Cannes 900004**
Circumnavigators' Club	**New York 6861227**
Club de la Bastide du Roy	**Nice 345027**
Diners' Club	**New York 2451500**
Explorers' Club	**New York 6288789**
Harvard Club	**Boston 5361260**
Hunting & Equestrian Club	**Kuwait 717271**
Islamabad Club	**Islamabad 22651**
Ja'afari Athletic Club	**Tehran 666885**
Jockey Club	**New York 3556146**
Karachi Race Club	**Karachi 515809**
Knickbocker Club	**New York 8386700**
Lions Club	**Tehran 274282**
Madras Gymnkhana Club	**Madras 84572**
Playboy Enterprises Inc.	**Chicago 7518000**
Racquet & Tennis Club	**New York 7539700**
Radnor Hunt	**Malvern 6449918**
Royal Bermuda Yacht Club	**Hamilton 6144**
Royal Bombay Yacht Club	**Bombay 211011**
Royal Scottish Automobile Club	**Glasgow 2213850**
Sierra Club	**San Francisco 9818634**

Variety Clubs	
International	**New York 7518600**
Woodlands Sun &	
Health Club	**Sydney 6065498**
Workmen's Club	**Dublin 751192**
Yale Club	**Philadelphia 7357619**

ACTS OF UNION
20 world trade unions

There are two names you won't find in this list. One is Solidarity, not long ago the world's largest union, which was disbanded. The other is the International Association of Marble, Slate and Stone Polishers, Rubbers and Sawyers, Tile and Marble Setters Helpers and Marble, Mosaic and Terrazzo Workers Helpers of Washington DC, which is too much of a mouthful. Here are the more manageable ones . . .

Associated Actors and	
Artists of America	
(AAAA)	**New York 8690358**
Brotherhood of	
Maintenance of	
the Way	
Employees	**Detroit 8680492**
Confédération Générale	
du Travail	**Paris 2088650**
Confédération Générale	
du Travail du	
Luxembourg	**Luxembourg 486949**
Confederazione	
Generale Italiana	
del Lavoro	**Rome 841021**

Deutscher Gewertschaftsbund	**Düsseldorf 43011**
European Trade Union Confederation	**Brussels 2179141**
Fédération Générale du Travail de Belgique	**Brussels 5116466**
General Council of Trade Unions of Iapan	**Tokyo 4332211**
Hebrew Actors' Union	**New York 6741923**
International Federation of Plant Agricultural and Allied Workers	**Geneva 313105**
International Labour Organization	**Geneva 326200**
Irish Congress of Trade Unions	**Dublin 680641**
Israel Farmers' Federation	**Tel Aviv 252227**
Landsorganisasjonen i Norge	**Oslo 206770**
Landsorganisationen i Danmark	**Copenhagen 353541**
National Union of Mineworkers	**London 3877631**
Professional Rodeo Cowboys Association	**Denver 4553270**
Trades Union Congress	**London 2622401**
World Federation of Trade Unions	**Prague 67856**

AIRLINES
50 of the world's national carriers

Air travel, they tell us, is the safest way on earth of getting from A to B; the only problem being, the critics reply, that the earth doesn't have much to do with the process except for providing somewhere to ι nd, or occasionally crash. If you are among the number who have a horror of leaving terra firma, then you'll share Al Boliska's point of view that 'Airline travel is hours of boredom interrupted by moments of stark terror', and you'll want to minimize both by contacting . . .

Aer Lingus	**Dublin 370011**
Aerolinea Argentinas	**Buenos Aires 302071**
Air Canada	**Montreal 87414560**
Air France	**Paris 2734141**
Air India	**Bombay 23142**
Air New Zealand	**Auckland 78919**
Alia	**Amman 22314**
Al Italia	**Rome 54441**
American Airlines	**New York 5571234**
Ariana Afghan Airlines	**Kabul 25541**
Balkan Bulgarian Airlines	**Sofia 451121**
Cubana Airlines	**Havana 74911**
Delta Airlines	**Atlanta 7622531**
Eastern Airlines	**Miami 8732211**
Egyptair	**Cairo 65136**
El Al	**Tel Aviv 976111**
Ethiopian Airlines	**Addis Ababa 52222**
Finnair	**Helsinki 410411**
Ghana Airways	**Accra 64851**
Iberia International Airlines	**Madrid 2619100**
Icelandair	**Reykjavik 27800**

Japan Airlines	**Tokyo 2852081**
Kenya Airways	**Nairobi 29231**
KLM	**Amsterdam 499123**
Korean Airlines	**Seoul 288231**
Libyan Arab Airlines	**Tripoli 36021**
Lufthansa	**Cologne 8261**
Malaysian Airline System	**Kuala Lumpur 208811**
Nigeria Airways	**Lagos 31031**
Olympic Airways	**Athens 0219291**
Pakistan International Airlines	**Karachi 412611**
Pan American	**New York 9737700**
Polish Airlines (LOT)	**Warsaw 461251**
Qantas	**Sydney 2300699**
Royal Air Maroc	**Casablanca 364184**
Sabena	**Brussels 5119060**
Saudia	**Jeddah 5141**
Scandinavian Airlines	**Stockholm 7801000**
Singapore Airlines	**Singapore 2821111**
South African Airways	**Johannesburg 237424**
Sudan Airways	**Khartoum 76411**
Swissair	**Zurich 8121212**
TAA	**Melbourne 3451333**
Thai Airways International	**Bangkok 72040**
Turkish Airlines	**Istanbul 462050**
TWA	**New York 5573000**
United Airlines	**Chicago 9524000**
Varig Brazilian Airlines	**Rio de Janeiro 2225141**
Yugoslav Airlines (JAT)	**Belgrade 683299**
Zambia Airways	**Lusaka 51214**

AIR SUPREMACY
25 national air forces

Lord Kelvin, President of the Royal Society as recently as the 1890s, proved that it was impossible to fly in a heavier-than-air machine, and while Frank Whittle was working on his prototype jet engine before the last war, the Professor of Aeronautical Engineering at Cambridge reputedly looked at his design and immediately dismissed it with the remark, 'Very interesting, Whittle, my boy, but it will never work.' History proved both of them some way short of the mark, and even if the US air force did consist only of fifty men at the outbreak of the First World War, the matter has been rectified since then. For further details ring . . .

Australian air force	**Canberra 659111**
Belgian air force	**Brussels 2162180**
Czech air force	**Prague 098**
Finnish air force	**Tikkakoski 751322**
French air force	**Paris 8287090**
German air force	**Bonn 121**
Guatemalan air force	**Guatemala City 64081**
Honduran air force	**Tegucigalpa 2309**
Indian air force	**New Delhi 370231**
Japanese air force	**Tokyo 4085211**
Kenyan air force	**Nairobi 50361**
Lebanese air force	**Beirut 420400**
Netherlands air force	**The Hague 814321**
Norwegian air force	**Oslo 178080**
Polish air force	**Warsaw 82031**
Portuguese air force	**Lisbon 972383**
South African air force	**Pretoria 29541**
Spanish air force	**Madrid 4497000**
Swedish air force	**Stockholm 679500**

Turkish air force	**Ankara 110310**
Ugandan air force	**Kampala 2251**
UK, Royal Air Force	**London 2189000**
US air force	**Washington DC 6954803**
Zambian air force	**Lusaka 51033**
Zimbabwean air force	**Causeway 794861**

AIRWAVES
20 radio networks

'The ideal voice for radio,' said Ed Murrow over thirty years ago, 'should have no substance, no sex, no owner, and a message of importance for every housewife.' Sadly this is no longer the case, but as most radio networks seem to enjoy hearing from the people who hear them, it might be worth reviving this old ideal, in which case try . . .

ABC	**Sydney 310211**
American Forces Network	**Burggaben 3101866**
Bahamas Broadcasting & Television Commission	**Nassau 24623**
Canadian Radio-Television & Telecommunications Commission	**Ottawa 9970313**
Corporation Panemana de Radiofusion	**Panama City 250160**
Danmarks Radio	**Soeburg 671233**
Downtown Radio	**Newtownards 815555**
Guyana Broadcasting	**Georgetown 2691**

Nicholson's Broadcasting Services	Perth 253311
Radio Americas	Mayaguez 8321150
Radio & Télévision France	Paris 2242222
Radio Europe No 1	Saarbrucken 31301
Radio Free Europe	Munich 21021
Radio Luxembourg	Luxembourg 47661
Radio New Zealand	Wellington 721777
Radio Telefis Eireann	Dublin 693111
Radio-Télévision-Belge	Brussels 359060
Rediffusion	Port-of-Spain 21151
South African Broadcasting Corp	Johannesburg 7140111
Sveriges Radio	Stockholm 631000

ALL AT SEA
12 shipping companies

When Noah went into the shipping business, he did so in a big way. The ark, built by Noah & Sons, measured twice the length of Nelson's flagship *Victory*, though after its maiden voyage Noah pulled out of the sea business, leaving the field open to later arrivals like . . .

British and Common- wealth Shipping Co	**London 2824343**
Bruusgaard Kiøsteruds Skibsaksjeselskap	**Drammer 838670**
Compagnie auxilliare de Navigation	**Paris 8749950**
Compagnie Générale Transatlantique	**Paris-La-Défense 7751411**
Cunard Steam Ship Co	**London 7411644**
DDG Hansu Det Bergenske Dampskibssel- skab	**Bergen 210020**
Furness, Withy & Co	**London 4812525**
Koninklijke Nedland Groep	**Rotterdam 1779**
London & Overseas Freighters	**London 4994941**
Nippon Yuseh Kaisha	**Tokyo 4545111**
Peninsular and Oriental Steam Navigation Co	**London 2838000**
World Wide Shipping Agency	**Hong Kong H-242111**

ALL THAT GLITTERS
15 world jewellers and gem suppliers

Remember that whopping diamond that Richard Burton
gave Liz Taylor back in 1972? His comment on it was
suitably dismissive, 'This diamond has so many carats, it's
almost a turnip.' If you fancy another like it, you might try
ringing Cartier's to see if they can oblige. On the other hand
a phone call to Tehran 310101 might be worth a shot

Rumour has it they're clearing out some of the Shah's booty and this used to be the number for the Imperial Crown Jewels.

Astwood-Dickinson	**Hamilton 11205**
British Crown Jewels	**London 7090765**
Cartier	**New York 7530111**
Coro	**New York 9471329**
Essex Jewellery	**Montreal 2882216**
Fremes	**Toronto 3634158**
Hammer Galleries	**New York 7580409**
Kamin & Co	**Melbourne 634320**
Maliram Puranmal Rawat	**Jaipur 72866**
Manzo Park Lane	
Diamonds	**Sydney 265080**
Ming's	**Honolulu 5361757**
Paswal	**Bon Juan 7425424**
Richter's	**New York 3554600**
Spritzer & Fuhrman	**Willemstad 12600**
Wright's	**Kingston 9223264**

ALL THE PERFUMES OF ARABIA
or 8 from just about anywhere else

The world's most expensive perfume will set you back about £200 an ounce, but if your tastes are more modest you might care to telephone the following to see how they compare . . .

Cécile Maison Française	**Hamilton (Bermuda) 15896**
Cox	**Sydney 927649**
Fabergé	**New York 5813500**
Herdt & Charton	**Montreal 2594641**
Houbigant	**Ridgefield 9413400**

Norda International	**Slough 26864**
Shairi Industries	**Lucknow 82631**
Shama Banerji	**Calcutta 562428**

ALL THE WORLD'S A STAGE
20 world theatres

The world's largest theatre has seating capacity for 10,000; its smallest can accommodate a mere thirty patrons. As it happens, neither of these appears in the list below because getting seats is tricky in both cases. One is in Peking and is only used as a theatre infrequently; the other is in Hamburg and sells out without difficulty. You stand a better chance in the rest, however.

Aarhus Theater	**Aarhus 120572**
Arts Theatre	**Cambridge 5200**
Central Puppet Theatre	**Moscow 2995430**
Comédie Française	**Paris 2961020**
Gate Theatre	**Dublin 767609**
Greek Art Theatre	**Athens 3222760**
McCormick Place and Arie Crown Theater	**Chicago 7916000**
Municipal Auditorium	**New Orleans 5258441**
National Theatre	**London 9282033**
New York Shakespeare Festival	**New York 6771750**
Nimrod Theatre	**Sydney 6995003**
Oscars Teatern	**Stockholm 234700**
Royal Shakespeare Co	**Stratford-upon-Avon 3693**
Royal Theatre	**Copenhagen 01141766**
San Carlo Theater	**Lisbon 368408**
Teatr Narodwy	**Warsaw 270668**

Teatro della Pergola	**Florence 262690**
Théâtre National du Palais de Chaillot	**Paris 7278115**
Théâtre Royal de la Monnaie	**Brussels 172211**
Young Vic	**London 6330133**

ALL TOGETHER NOW
18 international agencies

International organizations have come in for their fair share of stick; here's Ken Tynan on the Common Market. 'I do not see the EEC as a great love affair. It is more like nine middle-aged couples with failing marriages meeting at a Brussels hotel for a group grope.' There's no getting away from the importance they have in our lives, though, and working on the principle that if you can't beat 'em, join 'em, here are some to get your teeth into . . .

American Association for the Advancement of Science	**Washington DC 4674400**
Commission for the European Communities	**Brussels 7350040**
Council of Europe	**Strasbourg 357035**
Economic Commission for Western Asia	**Amman 63163**
European Space Research & Technology Centre	**Noordwijk 86555**
International Civil Service Commission	**New York 7548465**
International Commission of Jurists	**Geneva 493545**
International Court of Justice	**The Hague 392344**

18

League of Arab States	**Cairo 811960**
NATO	**Brussels 410040**
Nobel Foundation	**Stockholm 630920**
OECD	**Paris 5248200**
OPEC	**Vienna 639780**
Organization of African Unity	**Addis Ababa 47480**
United Nations Social Defence Research Unit	**Rome 655301**
War Resisters' International	**London 8373860**
World Future Society	**Betheseda 6568274**
World Intellectual Property Organization	**Geneva 346300**

ARTISTIC LICENCE
20 painters and other artists

Modern art doesn't suit all tastes. 'Abstract Art,' wrote Al Capp, is 'a product of the untalented, sold by the unprincipled to the utterly bewildered.' For the complete picture you should contact . . .

Andersen, Mogens	**Copenhagen 620266**
Annigoni, Pietro	**Florence 212438**
Bernáth, Aurél	**Budapest 325524**
Blume, Peter	**Sherman 3547429**
Brauer, Erich	**Vienna 347160**
Brayer, Yves	**Paris 0330001**
Chapelain-Midy, Roger	**Paris 7072790**
Christo	**New York 9664437**
Erni, Hans	**Lucerne 371382**

19

Hayter, Stanley	**Paris 3262660**
Heron, Patrick	**Penzance 796921**
Knapp, Stefan	**Wormley 2430**
Levine, Jack	**New York (Yukon) 95900**
Masson, Marcel	**Paris 8784239**
Plattner, Karl	**Milan 875927**
Sotomayer, Antonio	**San Francisco 6736193**
Spyropolous, Jannis	**Athens 281182**
Ten Holt, Frisco	**Amsterdam 230736**
Venzo, Mario	**Varese 796167**
Warhol, Andy	**New York 4755550**

ARTS COUNSEL
or culture at your fingertips

You may never have heard of Giotto or Nagasawa Rosetu, let alone be on a nodding acquaintance with their work. All that matters is that you keep your ignorance, or indifference, to yourself. There's no need to be a culture vulture either. A few slips of paper left lying about strategically with a few scrawled numbers will work wonders with anyone who fancies himself a connoisseur. Here are some to be getting on with.

Art Gallery of Ontario	**Toronto 3610414**
Art Gallery of South Australia	**Adelaide 2238911**
Centre National d'Art et de Culture G. Pompidou	**Paris 2771233**
Ceskoslovenské středisko výtamych oměni	**Prague 220652**
Galleria degli Uffizi	**Florence 218341**
Galleria Nazionale delle Marche	**Urbino 2760**
Galleria Palatina	**Florence 260695**

Grand Rapids Art Museum	**Grand Rapids 4594676**
Jehangir Art Gallery	**Bombay 257797**
Metropolitan Museum of Art	**New York 8795500**
Musée des Beaux Arts	**Beirut 25285**
Musée des Beaux Arts	**Marseille 547775**
Museo Picasso	**Barcelona 3196902**
National Art Gallery of New Zealand	**Wellington 859703**
National Gallery	**London 8393321**
National Gallery of Canada	**Ottawa 9924636**
National Gallery of Ireland	**Dublin 767571**
National Gallery of Victoria	**Melbourne 627411**
National Gallery of Zimbabwe	**Grahamstown 704666**
Queensland Art Gallery	**Brisbane 292138**
Royal Academy of Arts	**London 7349052**
South African National Gallery	**Cape Town 451628**
Staatliche Kunstammlingen	**Dresden 44611**
Statens Museum for Kunst	**Copenhagen 112126**
Tate Gallery	**London 8217128**
Tokyo Metropolitan Art Museum	**Tokyo 8236921**

ATOM SMASHING
7 nuclear agencies

As Bennett Cerf sagely remarked, 'The Atomic Age is here to stay – but are we?' For the answer to this and similar questions, telephone . . .

American Nuclear Society	**Hinsdale 3251991**
Energie Froide International	**Geneva 4776655**
Euratom (Communauté Européene de l'Energie Atomique)	**Brussels 358040**
International Atomic Energy Agency	**Vienna 524511**
Nuclear Data	**Palatine 5294600**
Nuclear Regulatory Commission	**Bethesda 4927000**
Oak Ridge Atom Industries	**Varese 9688575**

BACK NUMBERS
30 world periodicals from cricket to courting

For a time *Life* magazine numbered among its staff a Mr Yi, a journalist of no mean talent, who later left his post to take up a more exalted position in diplomatic circles. During his spell on the magazine, he was often the receiver of telephone calls which went along the lines of, 'Hello, Yi speaking,' to which the gleeful caller would reply, 'Ah, sweet Mr Yi of *Life*.'

Australian Cricket	**Sydney 334282**
Australian Hot Rod	**Sydney 6997861**
British-Soviet Friendship	**London 2534161**
Charmaine	**Durban 422041**
Cosmetic World News	**London 4866757**
Cosmopolitan, UK	**London 4397144**
Cosmopolitan, USA	**New York 2625700**
Country Life	**London 2617058**
Dalhousie Review	**Halifax 4242541**
Ebony	**Chicago 7867600**
Eve's Weekly	**Bombay 271444**
Glamour Girl	**New York 6925500**
Harper's & Queen	**London 4397144**
Men Only	**London 7349191**
National Lampoon	**New York 6884070**
Penthouse	**New York 5933301**
Playboy	**Chicago 7518000**
Pleisure!	**Accra 66640**
Port of London	**London 4766900**
Private Eye	**London 4374017**
Punch	**London 5389199**

Rooi Rose	**Durban 422041**
Saturday Night Magazine	**Toronto 3625907**
Sea Spray	**Auckland 689959**
Slimmer Magazine	**London 6912888**
Tatler & Bystander, The	**London 4937338**
Time	**New York 5861212**
Vogue	**New York 6925500**
Word, The	**Roscommon 7222**

BANK INTEREST
30 numbers to help you out of a jam or into the red

As the song says 'Money makes the world go round' and going round the world can sometimes make getting hold of money itself that much easier too. Take Indonesia, where for one penny you can get nearly 120 one-sen notes, for what they're worth. For something a little more durable and easier to carry, try the American 10,000-dollar bill. Though if you really want to go over the top there's always the Hungarian 100-trillion-pengö note, but this is a bit hard to come by. It was issued for just over a month in the summer of 1946!

Algemene Bank	
Nederlande	**Amsterdam 29911**
American Express	**New York 4802000**
Banca Central	**Madrid 2328810**
Banca Nazionale del Lavoro	**Rome 4661**
Bank of Baroda	**Agra 75363**
Bank of England	**London 6014444**
Bank Melli	**Tehran 3231**
Bank of New South Wales	**Sydney 2330500**
Bank Pars	**Shiraz 22391**
Bank of Tokyo	**Tokyo 2708111**
Banque Nationale de Paris	**Paris 5235500**

24

Barclays	**London 6261567**
Beogradska Bank	**Belgrade 624455**
Chase Manhattan	**New York 5522222**
Commerzbank	**Düsseldorf 8271**
Commonwealth Banking Corporation	**Sydney 20155**
Crédit Lyonnais	**Paris 2957000**
Crédit Suisse	**Zurich 2151111**
Dai-ichi Kangyo Bank	**Tokyo 2161111**
Danmarks Nationalbank	**Copenhagen 141411**
Hongkong and Shanghai Banking Corporation	**Hong Kong 222011**
Lloyds	**London 6261500**
Midland	**London 6269911**
National Bank of Australia	**Melbourne 630471**
National Bank of Greece	**Athens 3210411**
National Westminster	**London 6066060**
Rothschild & Sons	**London 6264356**
Royal Bank of Canada	**Montreal 8742110**
Wells Fargo	**San Francisco 3960123**
World Bank	**Washington DC 3936360**

BEER CALLER
40 ways to drink your way around the world

'There are two reasons for drinking,' wrote Thomas Love Peacock, 'one is, when you are thirsty, to cure it; the other, when you are not thirsty, to prevent it.' Thanks to the wonders of modern transport, we need never go thirsty. All one needs is a little spare cash, a timetable of world airline schedules and a quiet hour or two to plan the right itinerary. Armed with these no drinker need ever fear going without a pint It'll keep him out of trouble too, as Eden Phillpotts commented in *The Farmer's Wife*, 'Beer drinking don't do half the harm of lovemaking' – something about provoking the desire, but taking away the performance . . . ?

Allied Breweries	**London 2539911**
Anheuser-Busch	**St Louis 5770577**
Antiliaanse Brouwerij	**Willemstad 36442**
Bass Charrington	**London 8343121**
Bavaria	**Bogotá 321540**
Berliner Kundl Brauerei	**Berlin 620231**
Binding Brauerei	**Frankfurt 60651**
Birra Wührer	**Brescia 361361**
Brewery Egill Skallagrimmsson	**Reykjavik 11390**
Canadian Breweries	**Toronto 9214111**
Carling Brewery	**Cleveland 2311000**
Courage	**London 4077676**
Cra Uniao de Cervejas Angola 'Cuca'	**Luanda 80041**
Desnoes & Geddes	**Kingston 36421**
Dortmunder Union-Schultheiss Brauerei	**Dortmund 19171**
Grafton Brewing	**Grafton 422888**
Guinness	**Dublin 756701**
Heineken	**Amsterdam 709111**
Henniger-Bräu	**Frankfurt 60631**
Holstein Brauerei	**Hamburg 381011**
Joseph Schiltz	**Milwaukee 2245000**
La Constancia	**San Salvador 233000**
'La Victoria'	**Quito 211201**
Mohan Meaken's Brewery	**Lucknow 22422**
Molson's Brewery	**Toronto 8691786**
Pabst Brewing Co	**New York 2710230**
Rapid-American Corp	**New York 3994500**
St George Brewery	**Addis Ababa 47295**
San Miguel Brewery	**Hong Kong NT41311**

Schaefer Brewing Co	**New York 3877000**
Scottish & Newcastle Breweries	**Edinburgh 5562591**
South African Breweries	**Johannesburg 7241531**
South Australian Brewery Co	**Adelaide 513811**
Swan Brewing Co	**Perth 219161**
Three Horseshoes Brewery	**Breda 24241 .**
Toohey's	**Sydney 6488611**
United Breweries	**Copenhagen 211221**
Vaux Breweries	**Sunderland 76277**
Watney Mann	**London 8341266**
Whitbread	**London 6064455**

BEYOND THE GRAVE
dial-a-cemetery

Most people wanting to discuss a knotty problem in *Das Kapital* with the author would probably call on the services of a medium to tune in to Marx's wavelength. Few would consider dialling Highgate Cemetery on the off-chance that his spirit was paying a visit for old times' sake. It might be worth the price of a call nevertheless. Amy Semple Macpherson, a leading American spiritualist, had herself buried with a live telephone in her coffin!

Commonwealth War Graves Commission	**Maidenhead 34221**
Dublin Cemeteries	**Dublin 301133**
Forest Lawn Mausoleum	**Toronto 2253345**
Highgate Cemetery	**London 3401834**
Home of Peace Cemetery	**San Francisco 7512535**
Kensico Cemetery	**New York Enterprise 7348**
Northern Suburbs Cemetery	**Sydney 291326**

Pinnoroo Valley Memorial
Park   **Perth 3840018**

BIG BANG
explosives manufacturers

If you've ever had the inclination literally to get on the blower, or give someone a rocket, the following may be of some help.

Direction des Poudres	**Paris 2771570**
Dynamit-Nobel	**Troisdorf 5051**
Elgal	**Laurian 25343**
Filnobel	**Heraklion 288850**
Greek Powder & Cartridge Co	**Athens 3236091**
Nitro Nobel	**Gyttorp 25100**
Norsk Spraegnstodindustrie	**Oslo 410200**
Union Lorraine d'Explosif	**Nancy 533001**

BIN ENDS
18 vineyards, vintners and other wine producers

The French are the world's greatest wine drinkers with an average daily consumption of just under half a litre per head, which goes some way to explaining why a significant number of the entries below feature in French telephone directories.

Angove's	**Renmark 51311**
Anheuser & Fehrs, Weinkellereien	**Bad Kreuznach 28201**
Austin, Nichols & Co	**Hartford 8941234**
Barros, Almeida & Co	**Oporto 392104**
Bright Co	**Niagara Falls 3587141**
CDC Compagnie Générale des Produits Dubonnet Cinzano Byrrh	**Paris 5531540**
Champagne Pol Roger	**Epernay 514195**
Château Pavie	**Saint Emilion 247202**
Heidsieck, Charles	**Reims 401613**
Lindeman's	**Sydney 6470666**
Martini & Rossi	**Turin 531242**
Moët-Hennessy	**Paris 2615818**
Mumm, G.H. & Cie	**Paris 3593020**
Penfolds	**St Peters 550466**
Pernod Ricard	**Paris 5559255**
St Raphaël	**Paris 8874350**
Stellenbosch & Morris, The Stellenbosch Farmer's Winery	**Stellenbosch 2011**
Veuve-Clicquot-Ponsardin	**Reims 402542**

BIRDS OF A FEATHER
8 purveyors of plumage

Feathers; for the fan dance, the duvet or the next Ascot hat; we all have our own requirements and know what we want. Don't let yourself be given the bird by the retailers, get in touch with the dealers direct, phone . . .

British Feather Co Ltd	**London 6072213**
Fanghanel & Co	**London 3539637**
Feather Industries	**Toronto 7664142**
French Feather & Flower Co	**Montreal 8428511**
Missouri Flower & Feather Co	**St Louis 5551212**
Wallenstein & Schwartz	**New York 9472622**
Wilton's	**Sydney 461650**
Zucker, Nathan	**New York 9472653**

BLACK GOLD
25 oil companies

'If you can actually count your money, then you are not really a rich man,' said Paul Getty, who of all people knew most about the wealth tied up in oil. Anyone interested in the most up-to-date information should ring . . .

Ashland Oil	**Ashland 3293333**
BP	**London 9208000**
British National Oil	**Glasgow 2042525**
Burmah Oil	**Glasgow 2213793**
Compagnie Française des Pétroles	**Paris 5244646**
Esso	**Paris 7885000**

Exxon	**New York 3983000**
Getty Oil	**Los Angeles 3817151**
Gulf Oil	**Pittsburgh 2635000**
Indian Oil	**Bombay 453311**
Marathon Oil	**Findlay 4222121**
Mitsubishi Oil	**Tokyo 3311**
Mobil	**New York 8834242**
Murphy Oil	**El Dorado 8626411**
National Iranian Oil	**Tehran 6151**
Nigeria National Oil	**Lagos 21959**
Petrobrás	**Rio de Janeiro 2442477**
Royal Dutch Petroleum	**The Hague 776655**
Shell	**Houston 2416161**
Société Nationale Elf Aquitaine	**Paris 5786100**
Standard Oil (Indiana)	**Chicago 8566111**
Statoil	**Stavanger 33180**
Sun	**Radnor 2936000**
Texaco	**White Plains 2534000**
Ultramar	**London 6381757**

BLIND DATES
half-a-dozen escort agencies

Chérie	**Johannesburg 239547**
Dial-a-Girl	**Sydney 3571125**
Fantasia Massage & Escort	**San Francisco 5649933**
Fantasy Escorts East	**Newark 6225560**
Make-a-Date	**Toronto 9643366**
Prime Appointments Ltd	**London 4058824**

BLOCKING AND TACKLING
11 American football teams

'Nobody in football is worth a million dollars! It's ridiculous!'
exclaimed Joe Paterno, turning down a $1.3 million offer to
coach the Boston Patriots team. Anyone who disagrees with
this point of view might consider applying to . . .

Atlanta Falcons	**Atlanta 5881111**
Baltimore Colts	**Hunt Valley 6674400**
Buffalo Bills	**Orchard Park 6481800**
Dallas Cowboys	**Dallas 3698000**
Detroit Lions	**Pontiac 3354131**
Green Bay Packers	**Green Bay 4942351**
Miami Dolphins	**Miami 3791851**
New England Patriots	**Boston 5437911**
San Diego Chargers	**San Diego 2802111**
San Francisco 49ers	**San Francisco 4681149**
Tampa Bay Buccaneers	**Tampa 8702700**

BLUE BLOOD
a score of aristocrats

'A good family,' wrote Cleveland Amory, 'is one that used to
be better', a point which would no doubt be hotly contested
by . . .

Abergavenny, Marquess of	**Tunbridge Wells 27378**
Atholl, Duke of	**Blair Atholl 212**
Chaumbre, Comte de	**Paris 7226516**
Desazars de Montgailhard, Baron	**Paris 5631100**
Devonshire, Duke of	**Baslow 2204**
Harrington, Earl of	**Limerick 96129**

Howard de Walden, Lord	**Kintbury 229**
Iveagh, Lord	**London 8394296**
Marchwood, Viscount	**Cholderton 200**
Norfolk, Duke of	**Arundel 882173**
Portman, Viscount	**Clifford 235**
Posson, Baron de	**Le Zoute 61317**
Rothschild, Baron de	**Deauville 880407**
Roxburghe, Duke of	**Kelso 2288**
Strathalmond, Lord	**Upper Basildon 216**
Tavistock, Marquess of	**Chevington 215**
Vivier, Marquis de	**Bordeaux 234623**
Von Oppenheimer, Baroness	**Bergheim/Erft 7966**
Zetland, Marquess of	**Richmond (UK) 3222**
Zuylen, Baron de	**Paris 2257614**

BODY BEAUTIFUL
tattoos around the world

Ninety-six per cent of the skin covering Mr Wilfred Hardy of Nottinghamshire is in its turn covered with tattoos, while a Canadian tattoo artist, 'Sailor' Joe Simmons, had 4,831 separate tattoos on his body. Anyone interested in following their example might care to ring . . .

Adventure Tattoo	**Toronto 3666773**
Amazing Skin Odyssey	**San Francisco 2397019**
Blue Lagoon Tattooist Studio	**Porthcawl 8998**
Hammond, Wally	**Sydney 8370805**
Jaguar, J.	**Harare 27241**
Jock Tattoo Studio	**London 8370805**
O'Conner, J.	**Auckland 773601**

33

BOOK CALLS
20 shops for easy reading and something a little more demanding

Jacqueline Susann has sold getting on for 25½ million copies of *Valley of the Dolls*. If you haven't already got a copy, you'd stand more than a sporting chance of finding one here. On the other hand, should your thoughts revolve in higher spheres, you may have difficulty in tracking down David Wilkins's Translation of the New Testament from Coptic into Latin; only 500 copies were printed. Mind you, they sold so slowly that the book remained in print for 191 years, so it's worth asking.

Alfi's	**Tehran 763760**
Al-Hilal	**Bahrain 253836**
Angus & Robertson	**Sydney 2901900**
Banana Inn	**San Francisco 3927378**
B. Dalton	**New York 3493560**
Dar-al-Uloom	**Riyadh 61234**
Down to Earth	**Perth 32119752**
Fadi	**Fujairah 22416**
Foyle's	**London 4375660**
Gideons International	**Foxrock 893590**
Hatchards	**London 4399921**
International Bookstore	**Dammam 41784**
Jashanmal & Sons	**Dubai 431735**
Keyvan	**Tehran 820324**
Khayat	**Kuwait 437579**
New Zealand Sunday School Union Book Shop	**Auckland 774059**
Oman Family Bookshop	**Ruwi 702850**
Other Books	**Toronto 9615227**
University Co-op	**Sydney 212211**
Yoga Bookshop	**Johannesburg 375980**

BOOK WORM
a score of the world's great and not so great libraries

As a rule libraries are pretty stationary. No one in their right mind would relish shifting all 78½ million items in the Library of Congress, but back in the 10th century one jolly Persian vizier moved about with his 117,000-volume library strapped to the backs of 400 camels. These beasts were trained to walk in the same order day after day, to make sure that the books stayed in alphabetical sequence. That's before the telephone arrived. Ordering books through mobile libraries has at least become easier in the last millennium.

Bayerische Staats-bibliothek	**Munich 21981**
Biblioteca Nazionale Centrale	**Rome 4989**
Bibliothèque d'Art	**Brussels 483495**
Bibliothèque des Arts	**Paris 7420251**
Bodleian Library	**Oxford 44675**
Boston Public Library	**Boston 5365400**
Bulawayo Public Library	**Bulawayo 60966**
Central Archaeological Library	**New Delhi 35759**
Det Kongelige Bibliothek	**Copenhagen 150111**
Harvard University Library	**Cambridge 4952401**
Illinois State Library	**Springfield 7825185**
Johannesburg Public Library	**Johannesburg 8363787**
Library of Congress	**Washington DC 4265108**
London Library	**London 9307705**
National Diet Library	**Tokyo 5812331**
National Library	**Reykjavik 13375**
National Library of Australia	**Canberra 62111**

National Library of
  Canada   **Ottawa 9959481**
Sepahsalor Mosque
  Library   **Tehran 363738**
Yale University Library   **New Haven 4368335**

BREAKDOWN SERVICE
9 places to turn for help when things get out of hand

Breakdowns happen when you least expect them. Everything
can be moving along like clockwork and suddenly, to
continue the metaphor, something snaps and you grind to a
halt. At times like this you need professional help . . .

All Manhattan Auto
  Repairs   **New York 3627470**
Amir Service   **Yazd 6041**
Analytical Psychology of
  Ontario   **Toronto 9617767**
Austin Garage   **Izmir 39780**
Firhill Service Station   **Edinburgh 4415815**
Hypnosis Centre   **Sydney 9775149**
Mt Wellington Highway
  Towing   **Auckland 576077**
Tow-in   **Johannesburg 8391623**
Whelan Motors   **Dublin 373362**

BULLS AND BEARS
20 world stock exchanges

Playing the investment game has always been a risky business and never more so than at the end of the 1920s. Between the beginning of September 1929 and the end of June 1932 a cool $74,000 million was wiped off share values on Wall Street. To avoid being stung like this again, punters have taken to keeping a wary eye on the market. To join their number you may be in need of these numbers . . .

American Stock Exchange	**New York 9386000**
Athens Stock Exchange	**Athens 3211301**
Dow Jones Report	**New York 9994141**
Dublin Stock Exchange	**Dublin 778808**
Hong Kong Stock Exchange	**Hong Kong 5234543**
London Stock Exchange	**London 5882355**
Melbourne Stock Exchange	**Melbourne 620241**
Mexico City Stock Exchange	**Mexico City 5104620**
Montreal Stock Exchange	**Montreal 8712432**
Munich Stock Exchange	**Munich 552898**
New York Stock Exchange	**New York 6233000**
Omaha Grain Exchange	**Omaha 3416733**
Oslo Stock Exchange	**Oslo 423880**
Rome Stock Exchange	**Rome 6791735**
Singapore Stock Exchange	**Singapore 70730**
Stock Exchange Reports	**West Germany 1168**
Sydney Stock Exchange	**Sydney 280421**
Toronto Stock Exchange	**Toronto 3636121**
Vienna Stock Exchange	**Vienna 633766**
Zurich Stock Exchange	**Zurich 271470**

CAFÉ OLÉ
9 spots to keep abreast of the beau-monde

Ampis Snack Bar	**Karachi 514832**
Café Bohemia	**Chicago 2638310**
Café Bulvar	**Istanbul 450753**
Café de la Tour	**Chicago 5271144**
Café de Paris	**Bangkok 38971**
Café Pierre	**New York 8388000**
Coffee House	**Lahore 55559**
Le Café	**Miami 8657651**
North Pizza Pantry	**Tehran 285765**

CALLS OF COMPOSITION
30 composers

'I occasionally play works by contemporary composers,' said Jascha Heifetz, 'and for two reasons. First to discourage the composer from writing any more and secondly to remind myself how much I appreciate Beethoven.' To get the other side of the picture, ring . . .

Arapov, Boris	**Leningrad 2938263**
Avidom, Menahem	**Tel Aviv 795512**
Badings, Henk	**Marrheeze 04957327**
Baird, Tadeusz	**Warsaw 174312**
Beck, Conrad	**Basel 250451**
Bennett, Richard Rodney	**London 7344192**
Bentzon, Niels	**Copenhagen (Fasan) 24**
Berger, Wilhelm	**Bucharest 503090**

Bernstein, Leonard	**New York 5808700**
Birtwhistle, Harrison	**London 4375203**
Boulanger, Nadia	**Paris 8745791**
Bush, Alan	**Radlett 6422**
Copland, Aaron	**New York 7573332**
Cruz, Ivo	**Lisbon 680646**
Daniel-Lesur, Jean Yves	**Paris 7274986**
Dutilleux, Henri	**Paris 3263914**
Frammell, Gerhard	**Heidelberg 40102**
Goehr, Alexander	**Cambridge (UK) 61661**
Harris, Roy	**Pacific Palisades 4547147**
Holliger, Heinz	**London 9375158**
Kadosa, Pál	**Budapest 181398**
Nezeritis, Andreas	**Athens 8673239**
Olsen, Poul	**Copenhagen 585800**
Orgad, Ben	**Tel Aviv 254122**
Petrassi, Goffredo	**Rome 3605028**
Sculthorpe, Peter	**Sydney 324701**
Seter, Mordecai	**Tel Aviv 47611**
Tal, Josef	**Jerusalem 228736**
Theodorakis, Mikis	**Paris 3261466**
Tippett, Sir Michael	**London 4371246**

CALL TO ARMS
15 defence ministries

As the Falklands War showed, defence ministries have a fine line in public relations. The British aren't alone in this; one US information officer in Vietnam, who was having a rough time parrying reporters' questions on recent US missions into Cambodia, finally produced this winning reply: 'Bombing, bombing, bombing. You always call it bombing. It isn't bombing, It's air support.' A call to one of the numbers below on a similarly ticklish point is likely to result in the same sort of response. Try the first one for instance . . .

Argentine Ministry of Defence	**Buenos Aires 469841**
Australian Ministry of Defence	**Canberra 652999**
Burmese Ministry of Defence	**Myoma 640**
Canadian Ministry of Defence	**Ottawa 2328211**
French Ministry of Defence	**Paris 5559520**
Ghanaian Ministry of Defence	**Accra 77621**
Irish Ministry of Defence	**Dublin 771881**
Israeli Ministry of Defence	**Tel Aviv 256111**
Korean Ministry of Defence	**Seoul 26021**
Singapore Ministry of Defence	**Singapore 637744**
Sudanese Ministry of Defence	**Khartoum 70742771**
Ugandan Ministry of Defence	**Kampala 57095**
UK Ministry of Defence	**London 2189000**
US Ministry of Defence, Pentagon	
(Army)	**Washington DC 6953241**
(Navy)	**Washington DC 6941183**

CARDINAL NUMBERS
10 cardinals

Seeing, as any of the reverend gentlemen below will tell you, is not believing. If it were, there would be considerable confusion among the Catholic population of the Philippines for their spiritual leader is none other than Cardinal Sin. You can ring him on Manila 481867, and the others on . . .

Antonelli, Ferdinando	**Rome 6987124**
Baggio, Sebastiano	**Rome 6540137**
Freeman, James	**Sydney 2323788**
Hume, George Basil	**London 8344717**
Marty, François	**Paris 5552600**
Oddi, Silvio	**Rome 3568957**
Parecattil, Joseph	**Cochin 32629**
Ribeiro, Antonio	**Lisbon 563901**
Rugambwa, Laurian	**Dar-es-Salaam 22031**
Ursi, Corrado	**Naples 449118**

CASINO ROYALE
or placing your bets

Casino	**Trouville-sur-mer 866413**
Casino	**Vittel 081235**
Casino de Paris	**Hamburg 233660**
Casino du Liban	**Beirut 242734**
Casino Municipal	**Cannes 393466**
Grand Casino Municipal	**Royan 050390**
Grand Casino	**Menton 357078**
International Casino	**Nairobi 56000**
Société du Cercle Casino Palais de Savoie	**Aix-les-Bains 351616**

CASTLES ON THE AIR
30 fortresses, or history at your fingertips

Everyone knows that an Englishman's home is his castle, but what about all the châteaux and schloss dotted about the rest of Europe, not to mention far-flung bastions in the rest of the world? Some are decidedly uninviting and a quick phone call before any prospective visit could save a wasted journey and spare hours of unwarranted misery.

Arundel Castle	**Arundel 883136**
Bamburgh Castle	**Bamburgh 208**
Belvoir Castle	**Knipton 262**
Berkley Castle	**Dursley 810332**
Blair Castle	**Blair Atholl 355**
Braemar Castle	**Braemar 219**
Carisbroke Castle	**Newport 3112**
Castel S. Angelo	**Rome 655036**
Cawdor Castle	**Cawdor 615**
Château Condom	**Condom 281528**
Château d'Ancy le France	**Ancy le France 165**
Château de Belfort	**Belfort 285296**
Château de Chantilly	**Chantilly 4570362**
Château du Colombier	**Alès 863040**
Edinburgh Castle	**Edinburgh 2299191**
Gwalior Fort	**Gwalior 328**
Hiroshima Castle	**Hiroshima 217512**
Inverary Castle	**Inverary 2203**
Leeds Castle	**Maidstone 65400**
Nagoya Castle	**Nagoya 324467**
Neuschwanstein	**Neuschwanstein bei Füssen 935**
Nymphenburg Castle	**Munich 23911**
Raby Castle	**Staindrop 202**
Schloss Brunegg	**Aargau 561144**
Schloss Eferding	**Eferding 592**
Schloss Lenzburg	**Lenzburg 516651**
Sudeley Castle	**Winchcombe 602308**
Tower of London	**London 7090765**
Warwick Castle	**Warwick 495421**
Windsor Castle	**Windsor 68286**

CHIPS OFF THE OLD BLOCK
15 sculptors

The world's biggest sculpture has been underway since 1948 and still isn't completed, which isn't surprising since it requires the removal of 6,250,000 tons of rock and is 561 feet high. For more portable works of art try . . .

Adams, Robert	**Headingham 60142**
Antes, Horst	**Karlsruhe 491621**
Bill, Max	**Zurich 526060**
Borsos, Miklós	**Budapest 357958**
Butler, Reg	**Berkhamsted 2933**
Cappello, Carmelo	**Milan 898457**

Caragea, Boris	**Bucharest 504786**
Fenton, Beatrice	**Philadelphia 8488587**
Frink, Elisabeth	**London 4391866**
Greco, Emilio	**Rome 324148**
Hauser, Eric	**Rottweil-Allstadt 6751**
Moore, Henry	**Much Hadham 2566**
Pátzay, Pál	**Budapest 364820**
Row Chowdhury, Devi	**Calcutta 472921**
Teshigahara, Sofa	**Tokyo 4081126**

CHOCOLATE SURPRISE
a dozen of the world's confectioners

The British with their notorious sweet tooth are the world's
top sweet-eating nation. The Swiss are reckoned to make the
best chocolate and, needless to say, the Americans have the
world's largest chocolate factory. The only ones who don't
seem to have much of a look-in are those who produce the
cocoa from which the chocolate was, or at least used to be,
made. So, if you're bored with the usual nibble, why not
branch out into something a little more exotic?

Cadbury Schweppes	**Birmingham 4582000**
Chocolat Tobler	
American Corp	**New York 7658586**
Favarger	**Versoix 551255**
Karff's Koninklijke	
Cacao-en-Choc-	
alaadfabriek	**Amsterdam 945335**
La India	**Caracas 893331**
Linda	**Akureyri 12800**
Lindt & Sprungli	**Kilchberg 912211**
Nestlé	**Croydon 6862222**
Nestlé	**Vevey 510111**
Rowntree Mackintosh	**York 53071**

Ward Chocolate	**Philadelphia 5357766**
World's Finest Chocolate	
Inc	**Chicago 912211**

CHORUS LINE
a dozen dancers and their agents

'My own personal reaction is that most ballets would be quite
delightful if it were not for the dancing,' commented one
disenchanted member of the audience, recorded with glee in
the *Evening Standard*. For a different, though no less partial,
point of view try . . .

Antonio	**Madrid 2562401**
Bortoluzzi, Paolo	**Brussels 6732958**
Cullberg, Brigit	**Stockholm 615838**
De Valois, Dame Ninette	**London 8765574**
Dowell, Anthony	**London 2401200**
Dudinskaya, Natalya	**Leningrad 2147172**
Gnatt, Poul	**Oslo 446710**
Graham, Martha	**New York 3976900**
Helpmann, Sir Robert	**London 2352235**
Nureyev, Rudolf	**London 4939158**
Park, Merle	**London 7489456**
Rukmini, Devi	**Madras 75836**

COALS TO NEWCASTLE
7 national telephone bodies

For anyone who is no great lover of Bell's invention, what
better way of demonstrating one's displeasure than getting in
touch with those responsible for its propagation?

American Telephone and Telegraph Co	**New York 3939800**
Ericsson, L.M. Telephone Co	**Stockholm 7190000**
General Telephone and Electronics Corp	**Stamford 3572000**
International Telephone and Telegraph	**New York 7526000**
Singapore Telephone Board	**Singapore 2807**
Società Finanziaria Telefonica	**Rome 8589**
Spanish National Telephone Co	**Madrid 004**

COIFFURE CONNECTION
10 hairdressers

Hairdressers are used to some pretty odd requests, so if you feel like experimenting with the latest in punk styling, don't feel abashed. Howard Hughes, by this time a notorious recluse, used to ring his hairdresser from hotel suites dotted all over the USA, demanding an immediate haircut. Not satisfied with this, he insisted that the man used three dozen combs each session and specified that the scissors should only be those made from German soligen steel. Mind you, Hughes was prepared to pay for this service, but if you're feeling flush and fancy a spree, the following may well oblige . . .

Buz Beez	**Johannesburg 6782530**
Custom Cutting	**San Francisco 5638867**
Cut Above, The	**Toronto 3639037**
Maison Prague Unisex	**Dublin 749789**
Mane Line	**London 7342242**

'La Poms'	**Auckland Hsn 65777**
Split-enz	**Sydney 2330351**
Vidal Sassoon, UK	**London 6290813**
Vidal Sassoon, USA	**New York 5359200**
Ye Olde Hair Inn	**Perth 3679348**

COLLECTORS' ITEMS
40 world museums

Henry Ford thought that history was 'Bunk' and Charles Kingsley, professor of modern history at Cambridge in the 1860s, resigned his chair with the observation that 'History is largely a lie.' All the same museums have flourished and now cover nearly every aspect of human life from wine to whips or so it would appear from the list below.

Acropolis	**Athens 3236665**
Alexander Monastery	**Jerusalem 284580**
Ashmolean Museum	**Oxford 57522**
Australian Museum	**Sydney 2212100**
Black Creek Pioneer Village	**Toronto 6616600**
Bowes Museum	**Barnard Castle 37139**
British Museum	**London 6361555**
Brunei Museum	**Bandar Seri Begawan 24565**
Delphi	**Delphi 82313**
Deutsches Museum von Meisterwerken der Naturwissenschaft & Technik	**Munich 21791**
Fitzwilliam Museum	**Cambridge (UK) 69501**
Flagellation Museum & Library	**Jerusalem 282936**

Ghana Museums & Monuments	**Accra 121653**
Imperial War Museum	**London 7358922**
Indian Museum	**Calcutta 239855**
Iraq Museum	**Baghdad 36121**
Kabul Museum	**Kabul 42656**
Kyoto National Museum	**Kyoto 5411151**
Madame Tussaud's	**London 9356861**
Mohenjodaro (Indus Valley)	**Mohenjodaro 6**
Musée National de Louvre	**Paris 2603926**
Musées Royaux d'Art et d'Historie	**Brussels 7339610**
Museo del Prado	**Madrid 4680950**
National Archaeological Museum	**Athens 8217717**
National Maritime Museum	**Stockholm 223980**
National Museum of India	**New Delhi 3844**
National Museum of New Zealand	**Wellington 59609**
National Science Museum	**Tokyo 8220111**
Nepal Museum	**Kathmandu 11504**
Olympia	**Olympia 21529**
Rijkmuseum	**Amsterdam 731221**
Sacred Monastery of the Lord's Configuration	**Meteora 22278**
Salzburger Museum	**Salzburg 43145**
Schweitzerisches Alpines Museum	**Bern 430434**
Smithsonian Institution	**Washington DC 6284422**
South African Railway Museum	**Johannesburg 7134550**
Sparta	**Sparta 28575**

Staatliche Museen ze	
Berlin	**Berlin 2200381**
Uganda Museum	**Kampala 41714**
Wine Museum of San	
Francisco	**San Francisco 6736990**

COLLEGE CONNECTIONS
40 academic institutions

Dial Bologna 272933 and you'll get through to Europe's oldest university. Dial Riyadh 29500 and you'll be speaking to the world's largest university with an ultimate capacity for housing 15,000 families. Calls to the other institutions may well be equally rewarding . . .

Alexandria University	**Alexandria 71675**
Arts and Science	
University	**Mandalay 659**
Assumption College	**Worcester 7525615**
Bologna, University of	**Bologna 272933**
Brigham Young University	**Provo 3741211**
California, University of	**Berkley 6426000**
Cambridge, University of	**Cambridge (UK) 358933**
Catholic Universi_y of	
Louvain	**Louvain 220431**
Columbia University	**New York 2801754**
Cornell University	**Ithaca 2561000**
'Cyril and Methodius',	
University of	**Veliko Tirnovo 2611**
Damascus, University of	**Damascus 15102**
Erasmus University	**Rotterdam 145511**
Hanoi, University of	**Hanoi 3222**
Harvard University	**Cambridge (US) 4951585**

Havana, University of	**Havana 73231**
Istanbul, University of	**Istanbul 224320**
Kalamazzoo College	**Kalamazzoo 3838497**
Karachi, University of	**Karachi 419291**
Karl Marx University of Economic Sciences	**Budapest 186850**
Kyoto University	**Kyoto 7512111**
Massachusetts Institute of Technology	**Cambridge 2532701**
Miami University	**Oxford 5292161**
Moscow State University	**Moscow 1392729**
Oxford, University of	**Oxford 56747**
Paris, University of	**Paris 75231**
People's Own University	**Islamabad 43591**
Princeton University	**Princeton 4523000**
Rio Grande, University of	**Rio Grande 21501**
Riyadh, University of	**Riyadh 29500**
Rupert Charles University of Heidelberg	**Heidelberg 531**
San Carlos of Guatemala, University of	**Guatemala City 480154**
Tajik State University	**Dušanbe 4603**
Tel Aviv University	**Tel Aviv 410477**
Trinity College	**Dublin 772941**
Vassar College	**Poughkeepsie 4527000**
Vienna, University of	**Vienna 427611**
Warsaw University	**Warsaw 261847**
Yale University	**New Haven 4364771**
Yeungnam University	**Yeungnam 9961**

CONSTRUCTION CALLS
20 world architects

An architect's life is not without its perils. As Frank Lloyd

Wright once remarked, 'The physician can bury his mistakes, but the architect can only advise his client to plant vines.' So to avoid disappointment when it's too late, why not get a few quotes in advance from . . .

Candilis, Georges	**Paris 3296170**
Christensen, Kai	**Copenhagen 110201**
Figini, Luigi	**Milan 650162**
Fuller, Richard Buckminster	**Philadelphia 3872255**
Hiort, Esbjörn	**Rungsted Kyst 868815**
Imai, Kenji	**Tokyo 4682708**
Kikutake, Kiyonori	**Tokyo 9419184**
Mokrzyński, Jerzy	**Warsaw 262683**
O'Gorman, Juan	**Mexico City 483919**
Piccinato, Luigi	**Rome 320374**
Pietila, Reima	**Helsinki 626852**
Roche, Kevin	**Hamden 7777251**
Romizez Vazquez, Pedro	**Mexico City 5954388**
Scott, Michael	**Dublin 760621**
Seidler, Harry	**Sydney 9221388**
Soriano, Raphael	**Tiburon 4350472**
Vago, Pierre	**Paris 5489591**
Vimond, Paul	**Paris 7205953**
Weese, Harry	**Chicago 4677030**
Zanuso, Marco	**Milan 4040312**

COUNTING TIME
30 of the world's speaking clocks

There's a clock, if you can call it that, which works off hydrogen and which is accurate to within one second in every 1,700,000 years, and there's a real clock in Denmark that's accurate to within half a second in every 300 years. Unfortunately neither of these splendid timepieces is readily accessible by phone. The following speaking clocks may suffice, however . . .

Addis Ababa **002**	Lisbon **15**
Amsterdam **002**	London **123**
Beirut **15**	Melbourne **6074**
Belgrade **95**	Milan **16**
Berlin **119**	Nassau **917**
Brussels **992**	Paris **0338400**
Bucharest **244800**	Rio de Janeiro **130**
Buenos Aires **113**	Rome **16**
Caracas **19**	San Juan **7249696**
Dublin **1191**	Singapore **381**
Frankfurt **119**	Stockholm **90510**
Geneva **161**	Sydney **2074**
Glasgow **123**	Taipei **117**
Hamburg **119**	Vienna **1503**
Johannesburg **923**	Zurich **161**

COURT CIRCULAR
the long arm of the law from Lagos to London

The law may be an ass, but plenty of lawyers have made a fat living from its exploitation, and occasionally from the exploitation of some of its practitioners. 'What do you imagine I am on the bench for, Mr Smith?' asked Judge Wills of the future Lord Birkenhead. 'It is not for me to attempt to fathom the inscrutable workings of Providence,' replied the young barrister. Trying to fathom the inscrutable workings of the world's legal systems is baffling enough today. To give yourself a head chance, why not make use of these contacts for starters?

Bankruptcy Information	Chicago 4355693
Federal Constitution Court	Karlsruhe 149312
Lord Chancellor's Department	London 2193000
Magistrate's Office	Soweto 8251061
Supreme Court	Lagos (Nigeria) 630992
Supreme Court	Singapore 360644
Supreme Court	Tokyo 5815411
Supreme Court	Washington DC 2523000

CROWNING GLORY
9 sources of hair and hairpieces

There are various ways of dealing with baldness and grey hair in others. You can try and cover up the blemishes, or you can simply ignore them altogether. When one customer asked the assistant in the hairdresser's, 'Have you anything for grey hair?' the man politely answered, 'Nothing but the greatest respect, sir.' Now that's salesmanship.

De Meo Bros	New York 2438512
Evergreen Co	Hong Kong H241244
Florid Hair & Wig Products	Kaohsiung 29742
Flourish Hair & Wig Products	Hong Kong H243520
Hair Again	New York 8321234
Kaohsiung International Wig Corporation	Kaohsiung 220740
Skye Products	Johannesburg 8345218
Sophisticut	London 7235714
Trendman	Dublin 710911

CURRENT AFFAIRS
9 suppliers of power

The energy released in the average hurricane is roughly equal to half the electrical energy used in the whole of the USA every year. For more conservative and down-to-earth supplies, contact . . .

American Electric Power Co	**New York 4224800**
Bayernwerk	**Munich 12541**
British Gas Corporation	**London 7237030**
Chubu Electric Power Co	**Nagoya 9518211**
Consumers Power Co	**Jackson 7881030**
Electricité de France	**Paris 7642222**
Electricity Council	**London 8342333**
Gaz de France	**Paris 7665262**
Pacific Gas & Electric Co	**San Francisco 7814211**

CURTAIN CALL
50 male stars of stage and screen and their agents

Shakespeare called them 'poor players' and with unemployment running the way it is many actors are literally that. There are, however, those fortunate few who've managed to rise above the bread-line. Those like the first name on the list who received £102,000 per episode for the long-running TV series *M*A*S*H!*

Alda, Alan	**New York JU65100**
Allen, Woody	**New York 2356000**
Bates, Alan	**London 4394371**
Beatty, Warren	**Los Angeles 2747451**
Bogarde, Dirk	**London 4931610**

Brando, Marlon	**Beverly Hills 2719144**
Bronson, Charles	**Los Angeles 2715165**
Brooks, Mel	**Los Angeles 2772211**
Brynner, Yul	**New York 5566000**
Burton, Richard	**London 2354640**
Caan, James	**Los Angeles 2747451**
Caine, Michael	**London 6298080**
Chamberlain, Richard	**Los Angeles 2737190**
Connery, Sean	**London 6298080**
Courtenay, Tom	**London 6298080**
Crawford, Michael	**London 4394371**
Curtis, Tony	**Los Angeles 2781690**
Cusack, Cyril	**Dublin 809707**
De Niro, Robert	**New York 6979680**
Douglas, Kirk	**Los Angeles 2745294**
Dreyfuss, Richard	**Tarzana 7050806**
Eastwood, Clint	**Burbank 8436000**
Finney, Albert	**London 6298080**
Gould, Elliot	**Los Angeles 5504000**
Heston, Charlton	**Los Angeles 2737190**
Hoffman, Dustin	**New York 4723738**
Hope, Bob	**Burbank 8412020**
Howard, Alan	**London 8392977**
Hudson, Rock	**Beverly Hills 2747451**
Kristofferson, Kris	**New York 4898027**
Lancaster, Burt	**New York 5565600**
McCowen, Alec	**London 2403086**
McKellen, Ian	**London 3747311**
Mason, James	**London 4993080**
Newhart, Bob	**Los Angeles 5504000**
Newman, Paul	**New York 4867100**
Nicholson, Jack	**Los Angeles 2785200**
Niven, David	**Los Angeles 2737190**
Pacino, Al	**New York 7561674**
Peck, Gregory	**New York 6440440**
Poitier, Sidney	**Beverly Hills 2747253**

Redford, Robert	**New York 4848736**
Reynolds, Burt	**Los Angeles 6526005**
Richardson, Ian	**London 6364550**
Savalas, Telly	**Los Angeles 5504000**
Sharif, Omar	**London 7349361**
Stallone, Sylvester	**Beverly Hills 2732192**
Travolta, John	**Los Angeles 2748518**
Voight, John	**Beverly Hills 5560221**
Welles, Orson	**New York 7580800**

DEATH WHERE IS THY STING?
half-a-dozen funeral parlours

Of all the great taboos we face death is number one. Hard as
we may try to ignore it, though, death's feather will strike us
all down sooner or later, so surely it's better to make at least

CO-OP FUNERAL SERVICE?

some effort to tackle it. Some prefer to compose their own epitaphs – it's just a pity that so few of them ever get into print. Dorothy Parker favoured, 'Excuse my dust'; W. C. Fields came up with, 'On the whole I'd rather be in Philadelphia'; and Clark Gable fancied 'Back to the silents'. It doesn't matter what plans you make, the important point is to make sure they're put into practice when things are taken out of your hands. A word in the right ear will work wonders when the time comes.

Carnegie Funeral Home	**Dublin 804340**
Chipper, Donald J. & Son	**Perth 3815888**
Co-op Funeral Service	**London 4785166**
Far East Funeral Home	**Toronto 9221181**
Garlick Funeral Homes	**New York 4652050**
Grieve, D. & Son	**Glenrothes 758262**

DEEP HEAT
half-a-dozen Turkish baths

Gladiator Health Studios	**Auckland 796154**
Kensington Karate Klasses	**Sydney 6621359**
Kumiko Massage & Baths	**London 7347982**
Marika Beauty & Health Studio	**Toronto 9214331**
Paris Health Club	**New York 7493500**
Venus Health Spa	**Berkley 8459271**

DOCTOR IN THE HOUSE
18 physicians and surgeons

In 1972 one of the more ambitious medical students at the University of Marseille pulled a gun on one of his tutors and shot him dead, explaining afterwards that the late professor was hampering his medical career. Then there was the equally tragic case of a Nigerian witch doctor who was given the death penalty for shooting one of his patients. It turned out that this victim was testing a bullet-proof charm. Medical advance has never been without its hazards, as many of the following will confirm.

Barnard, Christian (heart surgeon)	**Cape Town 551359**
Blanco-Cervantes, Raül (chest specialist)	**San José 212082**
Blaškovic, Dionýz (virologist)	**Bratislava 48337**
Blokhin, Nikolay (cancer specialist)	**Moscow 1118371**
Bucalossi, Pietro (cancer specialist)	**Milan 700510**
Central Doctors' Service	**Netherlands 425277**
Dahl-Iversen, Erling (surgeon)	**Hellerup 7820**
De Thé, Guy (cancer specialist)	**Lyon 758181**
Ewertsen, Harald (ENT)	**Virum 856100**
Foch-Anderson, Poul (plastic surgeon)	**Copenhagen 866516**
Hamburger, Christian (general practitioner)	**Copenhagen 633116**
Järri, Osmo (pathologist)	**Turku 17390**
Lozoya, Solis (paediatrician)	**Mexico City 5730094**

Nakayama, Komei	
(surgeon)	**Tokyo 2610661**
Sambasivan, G.	
(malariologist)	**Geneva 345250**
Spock, Benjamin	
(paediatrician)	**Rogers 6366044**
Tesauro, Giuseppe	
(gynaecologist)	**Naples 320421**
Verdan, Claude-Edouard	
(hand surgeon)	**Lausanne 203304**

DOCTOR LIVINGSTONE, I PRESUME?
14 of the world's explorers

Livingstone didn't have a telephone, of course. He had no
need of one. Besides, if Stanley had been able to get on the
blower and ask how things were going, much of the romantic
image surrounding the great men would have evaporated.
Today's explorers live in an age of ready and easy
communication. But even they can be notoriously difficult to
track down when the mood takes them.

Attenborough, David	**London 9405055**
Bonington, Chris	**Caldbeck 286**
Fiennes, Sir Ranulph	
Twisleton-Wykeham	**Lodsworth 302**
Fuchs, Sir Vivian	**Cambridge (UK) 59238**
Herzog, Maurice	**Paris 2976384**
Hillaby, John	**London 4354626**
Ingstad, Helge	**Oslo 142135**
MacLean Sir Fitzroy	**Strachur 242**
Maillart, Ella	**Geneva 464657**
Redon, Clare (Francis)	**Lymington 74664**
Rose, Sir Alec	**Havant 77124**

Stark, Dame Freya	**London 4934361**
Tenzing, Norgay	**Darjeeling 2161**
Thesiger, Wilfred	**London 3527213**

DRESS SENSE
15 couturiers (and others) to suit your style, if not your pocket

The world of high fashion isn't noted for its abundance of wit, but there are occasional flashes of brilliance. Take the guest at one diplomatic banquet whom the waiter covered in soup and who still had the presence of mind to rebuke the poor man, 'Don't darken my Diro again.' Or there was Coco Chanel who once commented, 'Saint Laurent has excellent taste. The more he copies me, the better taste he displays.' There's not a lot you can answer to that, so Chanel's number doesn't appear here. The others might be worth a call though.

Amies, Hardy	**London 7342436**
Chambre Syndicale de la Couture Parisienne	**Paris 2666444**
Ciganer, André	**Paris 2250912**
Courrèges, André	**Paris 2250832**
Couture Leon Gabay	**Brussels 353916**
Dior, Christian	**Paris 3598372**
Lanvin, Jeanne	**Paris 2651440**
Lapidus, Ted	**Paris 2255254**
Laroche, Guy	**Paris 2255766**
Levi-Strauss & Co	**San Francisco 3916200**
'Pepi' Kalliope Kokkinides	**Athens 736060**
Quant, Mary	**London 5848781**
Rouff, Maggy	**Paris 2256430**
Saint Laurent, Yves	**Paris 7237271**
Simonetta	**Paris 3595671**

EASY-RIDERS
20 car-hire numbers from Tehran to Tokyo

There's little point in finding out that you need an international driving licence in, say, China only to find when you arrive that there isn't a self-drive car to be seen. Likewise you'd be wasting your time remembering to drive on the left in Surinam if you'd got nothing to drive. Admittedly Surinam and the People's Republic of China don't feature on all that many itineraries, but some of these destinations just might, and if you're paying a flying visit to the Ayatollah Khomeini or Mrs Gandhi, you won't want to be late. Ring ahead and have a car waiting.

Airways	**Boston 5424196**
Arabian Car Rental	**Jeddah 33965**
Arac	**Vienna 243221**
Efes Rent-a-Car	**Izmir 33100**
Husain Ali Slaibikh	**Bahrain 25270**
Inex	**Belgrade 622361**
Jumaira Rent-a-Car	**Dubai 434934**
Kay	**Melbourne 3473322**
Kuperus	**Amsterdam 58790**
Marloc	**Casablanca 73737**
Pananghai Services	**Doha 25778**
Quoraini Transport	**Ahmadi 980554**
Rent-a-Car	**Tehran 243053**
Rentalauto	**Barcelona 2540482**
Shebari & Sons Car Hiring	**Abu Dhabi 41610**
Sita World Travel	**New Delhi 43103**
Sumer Cars	**Baghdad 92143**
Tokyo Nissan	**Tokyo 400978**

| Turk Turing | **Istanbul 407127** |
| Worldwide Rent-a-Car | **Sharjah 355547** |

ELECTRONIC CIRCUIT
20 hi-fi and other electrical world leaders

With the electronic revolution fast overtaking us we're right to feel a tinge of anxiety that one day computers might be able to do away with us altogether. It's at moments like this that it's comforting to recall Solomon Short's wise maxim, 'The human brain is the only computer in the world made out of meat.' In spite of all the latest gadgets we still have the edge when it comes to originality.

AEG - Telefunken	**Berlin 8281**
CBS	**New York 9754321**
EMI	**London 4864488**
GEC	**London 4938484**
General Electric	**Fairfield 7502000**
Grundig	**Fürth/Bay 7031**
Hitachi	**Tokyo 2121111**
IBM	**Armonk 7561900**
Matsushita Electric	**Osaka 9081121**
Nippon Electric	**Tokyo 4541111**
Philips' Lamps	**Eindhoven 732305**
Rank Organization	**London 6297454**
RCA	**New York 5985900**
Sanyo	**Osaka 9911181**
Sharp	**Osaka 6211221**
Sony	**Tokyo 4482111**
Texas Instruments	**Dallas 2382011**
Thorn Electric	**London 8362444**
Toshiba	**Tokyo 5015411**
Whirlpool	**Benton Harbor 9265000**

ENGINE NUMBERS
a dozen national railways

Trains have had a peculiar fascination for some women in Egypt ever since their first appearance in the country. It hasn't been unknown for women to lie face upwards between the rails as a train thundered overhead in the hope of conceiving a child. Others have tried lying face down for the opposite reason. More conventional assistance, for both conditions, is available on other pages. For those interested in the world's railways for their own sake, these numbers may be of use.

Amtrak	**Washington DC 4847220**
Austrian Federal Railways	**Vienna 5650**
British Railways Board	**London 2623232**
Finnish State Railway	**Helsinki 717711**
French Railways	**Paris 8787720**

Netherlands Railways	**Utrecht 359111**
Norfolk & Western Railway Co	**Norfolk 9814530**
Public Transport Commission of NSW	**Sydney 2198888**
South African Railways & Harbours	**Johannesburg 220224**
Swedish State Railways	**Stockholm 7622000**
Swiss Federal Railways	**Berne 601111**
Zimbabwe Railways	**Bulawayo 72211**

EUNUCHS IN A HAREM
8 critics

'Critics,' wrote Brendan Behan, 'are like eunuchs in a harem: they know how it's done, they've seen it done every day, but they're unable to do it themselves.' Or as Ken Tynan described them more prosaically, 'A critic is a man who knows the way but can't drive the car.' For the point of view of the critics themselves, try . . .

Bosquet, Alain	**Paris 3879676**
Brugman, Hendrik	**Bruges 331210**
Davie, Donald	**Nashville 2928598**
Kott, Jan	**Stony Brook 2466057**
Porter, Andrew	**New York 8403700**
Schonberg, Harold	**New York 8732619**
Servolini, Luigi	**Livorno 34444**
Swinnerton, Frank	**Cranleigh 3732**

EVERGREENS
or enjoying flowers without the bore of growing them

Artificial flowers have come a long way from the plastic daffodils that used to be teamed with various brands of soap powder a few years ago. To see just how far artifice has progressed towards the real thing, here are some of the world leaders in the field, so to speak.

Acorn Seed Co Ltd	**London 2541826**
Arnold Associates	**New York 8713300**
Artiflora	**Dublin 974062**
California Artificial Flower Co	**Providence 4671800**
Damascus Art Flowers Ltd	**Montreal 3841230**
Davie, Boag (Exports) Ltd	**Hong Kong H221001**
Ice Box Flowers & Gifts	**Toronto 3682695**
Missouri Flower & Feather Co	**St Louis 5551212**
William Fuss	**New York 6880350**

EYE, EYE
7 telescopes and observatories

Among the less auspicious moments in the history of astronomy was the visit made to the Mt Wilson Observatory in California by Mrs Einstein, whose husband was not unknown in the scientific field. In the course of her tour the senior astronomer explained the intricate workings of the mighty telescope and mentioned in passing that one of its main functions was to determine the shape of the Universe. 'My husband does that on the back of an old envelope,' was Mrs Einstein's only comment. Those in search of similar enlightenment might be interested in calling . . .

Frank P. Brackett Observatory	**Claremont 6268511**
Hale Observatories	**Pasadena 5771122**
Kitt Peak National Observatory	**Tucson 3275511**
Lowell Observatory	**Flagstaff 7743358**
Mount Washington Observatory	**Concord 3695365**
National Radio Astronomy Observatory	**Charlottesville 2967321**
Steward Observatory	**Tucson 7950061**

FAST FOOD
6 takeaways

Even the most colossal jumbo burgers pale into insignificance beside the mega-burger made for the centennial celebrations in Rutland, North Dakota. This monster weighed over 1½ tons and served 6,500 people. If your requirements are more modest and you happen to find yourself feeling peckish in one of these six places, try . . .

Di Muro Mariano	**Dublin 692666**
Fingers 'n' Forks	**Perth 3874761**
Henny Penny	**Sydney 720427**
Kentucky Fried Chicken, UK	**London 2546952**
Pick 'n' Eat Fast Foods	**Johannesburg 239604**
Yankee Doodle	**London 3779229**

FESTIVAL PHONE-IN
25 international art festivals

Art festivals and the trappings that go with them are frequently something of a mixed blessing. Sir Thomas Beecham, for instance, was no great lover of the Royal Festival Hall. On different occasions he described it as 'an inflated chicken coop' and 'like a disused mining shack in Nevada. Frivolous and acoustically imperfect.' Others have been a bit more charitable, and art festivals still stagger on in the face of mounting inflation and the recession. For further information telephone . . .

Aldeburgh Festival of Music & Arts	**Aldeburgh 2935**
Ballet and Opera Festival	**Copenhagen 144665**
Beethovenfest	**Bonn 830663**
Berlin International Film Festival	**Berlin 26341**
Cannes Film Festival	**Cannes 991111**
Cork Film Festival	**Cork 52221**
Edinburgh Festival	**Edinburgh 2264001**
Festival de Wallonie	**Mons 37174**
Festival of Montreux-Vevey	**Montreux 24471**
Fiera di Milano	**Milan 384636**

Helsinki Festival	**Helsinki 90659688**
Holland Festival	**The Hague 558700**
International Film Festival of India	**New Delhi 387667**
Karlovy Vary Film Festival	**Prague 223751**
Melbourne Film Festival	**Melbourne 3474828**
Moscow International Film Festival	**Moscow 2977645**
Promenade Concerts	**London 5898212**
Richard Wagner Festspiele	**Bayreuth 5722**
Salzburg Mozart Festival	**Salzburg 71511**
San Francisco Film Festival	**San Francisco 9288333**
San Sebastian Film Festival	**San Sebastian 424106**
Thessaloniki Film Festival	**Thessaloniki 220440**
Vienna Festival	**Vienna 579657**
Wexford Festival of Music & the Arts	**Wexford 22240**
Yehudi Menuhin Festival	**Gstaad 410955**

FIDDLING ABOUT
7 top violinists

In March 1975 Mark Gottlieb sat on the floor of the swimming pool at Evergreen State College, Olympia, USA and played Handel's Water Music on his violin. He was the first to succeed in playing in this unusual environment. The violinists listed below, though less adventurous perhaps, make up the deficit with their undoubted expertise.

Gumiaux, Arthur	**London 4864021**
Haendel, Ida	**Montreal 4897740**
Menuhin, Yehudi	**New York 2976900**
Stern, Isaac	**New York 5565600**
Suk, Josef	**Prague 299407**
Wilkomirska, Wanda	**Warsaw 175843**
Zukerman, Pinchas	**London 9352331**

FILM CALL
30 movie companies

One reviewer in *Time* magazine once wrote of James Cagney, 'He can't even put a telephone receiver back on the hook without giving the action some special spark of life', and Hollywood, for all its faults, has contributed a rich supply of emotional chest-expanders. Of course there are movie companies in other parts of the world too, but Hollywood – Dorothy Parker's 'Seventy-two suburbs in search of a city' – still has the edge, as a phone call to any of the following will show.

Allied Artists	**New York 5419200**
Alligator Films	**Brussels 765211**
Anglo-EMI	**London 4370444**
Canart Films	**Toronto 9236000**
Central Film	**Oslo 676393**
Columbia	**New York 7514400**
Compagnie Jean Renoir	**Paris 7042846**
Condor Films	**Zurich 269612**
Damaskimos & Micaelides	**Athens 623801**
Disney, Walt	**Burbank 8453141**
Eldorado	**Rome 678801**
EMI Elstree Studios	**London 9531600**
Films Marcau	**Paris 3596491**

Hammer	**Iver 651700**
Hanna-Barbera	**Los Angeles 8515000**
Hitchcock, Alfred	**Universal City 9854321**
Image Flow Centre	**Vancouver 7315611**
Israel Film Service	**Jerusalem 64951**
Jet	**Barcelona 2540303**
Merry Film	**Copenhagen 317121**
MGM	**Calver City 8363000**
Monty Python	**London 9350307**
Paramount	**New York 3336400**
Rank Film Studio Division	**Iver Heath 651700**
Scary Pictures	**Toronto 9250425**
Scimitar	**London 7348385**
Star Film	**Vienna 654529**
Twentieth Century Fox	**Los Angeles 2772211**
United Artists	**Los Angeles 6577000**
Warner Bros	**Burbank 8456000**

FINGERTIP CONTROL
10 top pianists and their agents

Liberace once made just under £50,000 for one night's performance in New York, and that was over thirty years ago. The record earnings of any classical concert pianist belonged to Ignace Paderewski – he made $5,000,000 during his career which ended in 1941. Among today's leading players are . . .

Barenboim, Daniel	**London 9352331**
Bishop-Kovacevich,	
Stephen	**London 2299166**
Brendel, Alfred	**London 9375158**
Cherkassky, Shura	**London 4864021**
Demus, Joerg	**Vienna 366238**
Katin, Peter	**Toronto 7663687**

Malcolm, George	**London 3525381**
Reynolds, Anna	**Richmond 8766164**
Salzman, Pnina	**Tel Aviv 261993**
Swann, Donald	**London 6224281**

FIRE!
50 numbers to raise the alarm to match the temperature

The word 'fire' causes confusion at its very mention, that's why it's so important to remain calm when you have to dial the emergency services. Even Shakespeare, when he got

carried away, could be disturbingly ambiguous. Take one of
the famous choruses from *Henry V* which opens 'Now all the
youth of England are on fire.' A modern rendering would be,
of course, 'Now all the youth of England are lit up.' True as
that might be, it offers a very different meaning to the one
intended. You can't be too careful in the heat of the moment.

Addis Ababa **01**	Los Angeles **0**
Amsterdam **66666**	Madrid **2323232**
Athens **199**	Manila **472220**
Auckland **111**	Melbourne **000**
Bangkok **13**	Milan **34999**
Barcelona **2535353**	Montreal **8721212**
Berlin **112**	Moscow **01**
Bogota **19**	Munich **112**
Boston **0**	Nairobi **999**
Buenos Aires **382222**	Nassau **911**
Caracas **113**	New York **0**
Chicago **0**	Paris **18**
Copenhagen **000**	Rio de Janeiro **2342020**
Dublin **999**	Rome **44444**
Düsseldorf **112**	San Juan **3432330**
Frankfurt **112**	Singapore **999**
Geneva **118**	Stockholm **90000**
Glasgow **999**	Sydney **000**
Hamburg **112**	Taipei **119**
Helsinki **005**	Tel Aviv **102**
Hong Kong **999**	Tokyo **119**
Johannesburg **999**	Vancouver **341234**
Kuala Lumpur **0**	Vienna **122**
Lisbon **322222**	Washington DC **0**
London **999**	Zurich **118**

FLIGHT INTERNATIONAL
10 world aircraft manufacturers

With all the fuss cooked up over the development costs of Concorde we're apt to forget some of the earlier aeronautical cock-ups that have befallen the industry in its past. Take the plane designed by the misguided Italian aristocrat, Count Caproni, which had nine multi-layered wings and eight engines. It never flew, save for a brief hop above the surface of the lake where it met its end, but as a floating home it showed potential. Present-day ideas on aircraft development should be passed on to . . .

Aérospatiale	**Paris 5244321**
Boeing	**Seattle 6552121**
British Aerospace	**London 9301020**
Fuji Heavy Industries	**Tokyo 3472340**
Kawasaki Heavy Industries	**Kobe 3417731**
Lockheed	**Burbank 8476121**
McDonnell Douglas	**St Louis 2320232**
Rockwell	**Pittsburgh 5652000**
VFW Fokker	**Dusseldorf 4494**
Westland Aircraft	**Yeovil 5222**

FOOD GLORIOUS FOOD
35 firms to help you keep the wolf from the door

Mother Hubbard's cupboard was bare. Oliver Twist asked for more. And even at the end of the seventeenth century half the people in England never touched meat. They all had the misfortune of living before the age of easy bulk-buying and, of course, the telephone. Now all manner of exotic fare is available for those willing to buy it. Florida rattlesnake (a great favourite in the Deep South), sharks' fin soup and the other sort made from birds' nests, these and thousands of other delicacies are at your disposal, not to mention the humdrum items with which we stock our larders and give ourselves obesity. (A word in your ear about the snakes, though. If you're ordering from Iraq, remember you can't have them for Sunday lunch; any other day of the week is fine, but you'd be breaking the law if you tucked into rattlesnake or cobra on Sunday.) All you need is your list, these numbers and you're away.

Associated British Foods	**London 4998931**
Beatrice Foods	**Chicago 7823820**
Bell	**Basle 239248**
Boussois Souchon Neuvesel Gervais Danone	**Paris 2262420**
Brooke Bond Liebig	**London 2486422**
Campbell Soup	**Camden 9644000**
Carnation	**Los Angeles 9311911**
Central Soya Co	**Fort Wayne 4228541**
Compagnie des Salins du Midi et des Salins de l'Est	**Paris 2659570**
Consolidated Foods	**Chicago 7266414**
Del Monte	**San Francisco 4424000**
FMC	**London 2355081**
General Foods	**New York 6832500**
Green Giant	**Chaska 4482828**
Gulf & Western Industries	**New York 3337000**
H. J. Heinz	**Pittsburgh 2375757**
Hershey Foods	**Hershey 5344200**
Industrie Buitoni Perugina	**Perugia 70741**
Kelloggs	**Battle Creek 9625151**
Kraft	**Glenview 9982000**
J. Lyons	**London 6032040**
Moringag Milk	**Tokyo 4560111**

Nabisco	**East Hanover 8840500**
Nestlé	**Vevey 510112**
Quaker Oats	**Chicago 2226881**
Rank Hovis McDougall	**London 8211444**
Reckitt & Colman	**London 9946464**
Snow Brand Milk Products	**Tokyo 3582081**
Spillers	**London 2485700**
Tate & Lyle	**London 6266525**
Unibel	**Paris 2655420**
Unilever	**London 3537474**
Union International	**London 2481212**
United Biscuits	**Isleworth 5603131**
United Brands Co	**Boston 2623000**

FOREIGN AFFAIRS
11 foreign ministries

According to Lloyd George, Neville Chamberlain 'saw foreign policy through the wrong end of a municipal drainpipe'; doubtless there are several present-day statesmen who fall into the same category. Should any of them spring to mind from this brief list, why not give them a call?

Austria	**Vienna 66150**
Belgium	**Brussels 5126650**
Denmark	**Copenhagen 113038**
France	**Paris 2603300**
Hungary	**Budapest 350100**
Iceland	**Reykjavik 25000**
Iraq	**Baghdad 30091**
Japan	**Tokyo 5803311**
Syria	**Damascus 331200**
United Kingdom	**London 2333000**
USA	**Washington DC 6329630**

FORGERS
13 of the heavies

Armco Steel	**Middletown 4256541**
Bethlehem Steel	**Bethlehem 6942424**
British Steel	**London 2351212**
Gillette	**Boston 42117000**
Guest Keen & Nettlefolds	**Warley 5583131**
Kawasaki Steel	**Kobe 2214141**
Krupp	**Essen 1881**
Nippon Steel	**Tokyo 2424111**
Scheider	**Paris 2603672**
Stahlwerk Rochling-Burbach	**Völkungen/Saar 06898**
Steel Co of Canada	**Toronto 3622161**
USINOR	**Paris 7446519**
Vöest-Alpine	**Linz 07222585**

FUTURE PERFECT?
horoscopes for every sign of the zodiac

Prediction is a risky business. The Decca Recording Company turned down one group in 1962 on the grounds that 'We don't like their sound. Groups of guitars are on the way out'; the group in question was The Beatles. Then there was the Munich schoolteacher who remarked to one of his ten-year-old charges, 'You will never amount to very much.' Albert Einstein proved him wrong. And when it comes to the number of times when the world should have ended, the list is almost endless. For those with boundless faith, and money to burn, these numbers are provided . . .

Aries (March 21 – April 19)	**New York 9365050**
Taurus (April 20 – May 20)	**New York 9365151**
Gemini (May 21 – June 20)	**New York 9365252**
Cancer (June 21 – July 22)	**New York 9365353**
Leo (July 23 – August 22)	**New York 9365454**
Virgo (August 23 – September 22)	**New York 9365656**
Libra (September 23 – October 22)	**New York 9365757**
Scorpio (October 23 – November 21)	**New York 9365858**
Sagittarius (November 22 – December 21)	**New York 9365959**
Capricorn (December 22 – January 19)	**New York 9366060**
Aquarius (January 20 – February 18)	**New York 9366161**
Pisces (February 19 – March 20)	**New York 9366262**

GET STUFFED
a quartet of taxidermists

In the spring of 1890, 180,000 mummified cats went up for sale in Liverpool. The auctioneers were at something of a loss when it came to disposing of them, so they were offered as fertilizer. The auctioneer, brandishing a dead cat as a hammer, sold them off in one-ton lots and the average price worked out at a tenth of a penny per cat. Taxidermy comes a little more expensive these days, as a call to one of the following will prove.

Australian Taxidermy Studio   **Sydney 9137763**

Graham Teasdale FZS
  (Barbot Studios)   **Rotherham 64351**
Kodiak Taxidermy   **New York 4636720**
New Zealand Taxidermy   **Auckland 376360**

GOGGLE BOX
25 television networks

According to Frank Lloyd Wright television was 'chewing
gum for the eyes', and, following the analogy, if you reach a
point when you need to spit it out, where better to aim than at
the networks responsible?

ABC	**Sydney 617406**
American Broadcasting Companies	**New York 5817777**
ARD-Deutsches Fernsehen	**Munich 38061**
Asian Broadcasting Union	**Sydney 617406**
ATN	**Sydney 8587777**
BBC	**London 7438000**
Belgische-Radio-en-Televisie	**Brussels 361010**
CBC	**Ottawa 7313111**
CBS	**New York 9754321**
Communications Satellite Corp	**Washington DC 5546000**
Finnish Broadcasting Co	**Helsinki 441141**
General Television Corp	**Richmond (Australia) 420201**
GTN (German Television News)	**Berlin 3045555**
IBA	**London 5847011**

International Press Tele-communications Council	**London 4052608**
International Tele-communications Union	**Geneva 346021**
Japan Broadcasting Corp	**Tokyo 5014111**
NBC	**New York 6644444**
Norsk Rikskringkasting	**Oslo 469860**
Queensland Television	**Mount Coot-tha 362333**
Radio and Television France	**Paris 5510886**
Radiotelevisione Italiana	**Rome 38781**
South Australian Tele-casters	**Gilberton 446991**
Swan Television & Radio Broadcasters Ltd	**Tuart Hill 349999**
TCN	**Sydney 43444**

GOING, GOING, GONE
20 of the world's top auctioneers

Have you a Rembrandt for sale, or a Vermeer? Maybe you've got your eye on a little Sung vase that would go well in the loo; or now that the children have started to learn the violin it's time they had a proper instrument to play and you just happened to notice a Stradivarius in good nick in the latest catalogue . . . ? Go on, treat yourself. What's a million or two where art's concerned?

Ashby's Galleries	**Cape Town 27527**
Boscher, Michell et Grossart, Antoine	**Paris 5484788**
Christie's	**London 8399060**
Dorotheum, Kunstabteilung	**Vienna 5285650**

82

MAN ON PHONE
BY
VINCENT VAN GOGH

Frankfurter Münz-handlung	**Frankfurt 727420**
Galerie Koller	**Zurich 475040**
Galerie Moderne	**Brussels 5139010**
Gramercy Auction Galleries	**New York 4775656**
Joel, Leonard	**Melbourne 672893**
Manawatu Trading Co	**Palmerston North 76079**
Martinjola	**Rome 689543**
Neumeister Münchener	**Munich 283011**
North & Co	**Dublin 774721**
Phillips	**London 6296602**
Salles de Ventes du Parc Palace	**Monte Carlo 306844**
Sotheby's	**London 4938080**
Subastros Madrid	**Madrid 2223034**
Svensk-Frankas Konstauktioner	**Stockholm 639310**

| Vendhuis van de Vereeniging der Notarissen te 's-Graven-hage | The Hague 600181 |
| Ward-Price Ltd | Toronto 9239876 |

GOLF LINKS

25 top courses to test your handicap and keep you up to par

Though a Scottish game, not all Scotsmen have a universal passion for golf. Novelist Eric Linklater numbered among the milder of the clan. 'All I've got against it,' he once wrote, 'is that it takes you so far from the club house.' Happily the courses mentioned below have club houses that make the round of eighteen holes worth the struggle – for those that bother to venture on to the course at all that is.

Berchtesgaden	Berchtesgaden 21003787
Braemar	Braemar 618
Cannes	Cannes 479539
Carnoustie Championship	Carnoustie 53249
Château D'Ardenne	Dinant 666228
Gleneagles Hotel Course	Auchterarder 2231
Grand/Ducal	Luxembourg 34090
Gstaad Course	Gstaad 42636
Helsingin	Helsinki 550235
Helsingör	Helsingör 212970
Kitzbühl	Kitzbühl 6370
Karlova Vary	Oslava Vrata 12536001
Lake Karrinyup	Perth 4775777
Las Palmas	Las Palmas 351050
Murrayfield	Edinburgh 4472411
Ness	Reykjavik 17930

Oberfranken	**Bayreuth 09228319**
Palmane	**Lagos (Portugal) 62961**
Playa Ravenna	**Palma 239246**
Rose Hill	**Sydney 6291101**
Royal Dublin	**Dublin 336346**
Royal Sydney	**Sydney 3714333**
Royal Troon	**Troon 311555**
St Andrews	**St Andrews 3337**
St Anne's Old Links	**St Anne's-on-Sea 723597**

GOOD SHEPHERDS
11 of the world's religious leaders

There was some debate whether the first entry should have been classified under Racehorse-owners or maybe Jet-setters, but as in either case he'd have been in a class of his own, it seemed more appropriate to include his name here.

Aga Khan IV, Prince Karim	**Paris 6338547**
Dimitrios I (Patriarch of Constantinople)	**Istanbul 239850**
Elias IV, Mowad (Patriarch of Antioch and All the East)	**Damascus 116329**
Goldstein, Rabbi Israel	**Jerusalem 36020**
Graham, Billy	**Minneapolis 3380500**
John Paul II, Pope	**Vatican 6982**
Runcie, Most Rev Robert	**London 9286222**
Ryan, Most Rev Dermot	**Dublin 373732**
Scharf, Kurt	**Berlin 8312600**
Strong, Most Rev Philip	**Wangarrata 215603**
Sung Myong Moon, The Rev	**New York 7305782**

GRAND PRIX
4 world-champion drivers

Emerson Fittipaldi was the youngest world champion when
he won the title in 1972 at the age of twenty-five and Jackie
Stewart holds the record for the number of Grand Prix
victories, twenty-seven in his eight-year career. The others
did pretty well too!

Brabham, Sir Jack	**London 9374343**
Fittipaldi, Emerson	**São Paolo 2110219**
Hunt, James	**London 6375377**
Stewart, Jackie	**Geneva 610152**

HAIRLINE
8 places to keep in trim

The average human scalp has 100,000 hairs, though as a rule redheads have fewer hairs than blondes or brunettes. Since the only sure way to prevent baldness is castration, stylists around the world are kept busy both cutting off unwanted hair and making the best of what some customers have left. Some would even quibble at the term 'stylist'. Sir Winston Churchill was asked by one barber which style he favoured to which he replied that a man of his limited resources couldn't presume to have a style. 'Just get on and cut it,' he told the man.

Chaps Hair Care for Men	**Sydney 2311091**
Jack the Clippers	**Dublin 909497**
Jingles	**Johannesburg 7831836**
King David Hair Styles	**Auckland 2748252**
Mike Aronousky's Custom Hair Styling	**San Francisco 7317026**
Snippers Men's Hair Design	**Perth 3214409**
Sweeney's Hairstyling for Men	**Toronto 9229863**
Truefit & Hill	**London 4932961**

HAIR OF THE DOG

15 world watering-holes to slake your thirst and forget your troubles . . . and wake up with double measures of both

'I must get out of these wet clothes and into a dry martini,' once commented the American wit Alexander Woollcott, a remark that warms any drinker's heart. Hearts have a way of getting out of hand (if you'll pardon the anatomical

complexities) and when they do it's largely the head that suffers. Woollcott's fellow countryman, W. C. Fields, spoke for all when he made an equally telling reply on being offered assistance by one barman, 'Shall I fix you a bromo?' 'No,' said Fields, 'I couldn't stand the 'noise.' Who's to say what pleasures and perils lie in wait in this list; who indeed? But imagine the fun in finding out . . .

Atlantic Bar	**Bucharest 162936**
Bamboo Bar	**Bangkok 39920**
China Bar	**Addis Ababa 43014**
Femina Bar	**Vienna 631526**
Folies Berjer	**Istanbul 449569**
Grand Pub	**Osaka 3348281**
Horseshoe Bar	**Dublin 766471**
Milk Bar	**Shiraz 26163**
Oil Can Harry's	**Vancouver 6837306**
Penthouse Bar	**Singapore 371666**
Pyramid Bar	**Cairo 811811**
Roman Pub	**New York 5867000**
Sunset Club	**Lima 229874**
Swiss Inn	**Bangkok 51555**
Top of the Carlton	**Johannesburg 218911**

HAUTE CUISINE
30 of the world's great restaurants

The founder of the McDonald's hamburger chain is well qualified in his profession - he holds the degree of BH (Bachelor of Hamburgerology). For the qualifications of the men in charge of the establishments on this list, you'll have to make your own enquiries, though a call to Oak Brook 8873200 shouldn't be necessary.

Bagatelle	**Athens 730349**
Baku	**Moscow 998094**
Bucur	**Bucharest 136054**
Buena Vista	**Nassau 22811**
Caesar's Palace	**Tokyo 5844481**
Cattleman's	**Toronto 3684823**
Le Coq d'Or	**Kuala Lumpur 83522**
Doyles on the Beach	**Sydney 3372007**
Fauquet's	**Paris 2255954**
Howard Johnsons	**Braintree 8482350**
Kwality Restaurant	**Lucknow 23331**
Las Lanzas	**Madrid 2305079**
Lobster Pot	**Nairobi 20491**
McDonald's	**Oak Brook 8873200**
Manny Wolf's	**New York 3559020**
Maxim's	**Karachi 516588**
Maxim's	**Paris 2652794**
Mei Kong	**Lahore 83101**
Ratweinkellerei	**Hamburg 345683**
Ravenstein	**Brussels 5127768**
Red Coach Grill	**Miami 3794008**
Rissani	**Casablanca 7973233**
Ron	**Osaka 3626664**
Sandy's	**Tehran 891530**
Savini	**Milan 898343**
Simpsons	**London 8369112**
Steakhouse	**Istanbul 442619**
Tail o'the Cock	**Los Angeles 2731200**
Ting Li Kwan (Summer Palace)	**Peking 281936**
Troisgros, Jean	**Roanne 716697**

HEAVYWEIGHTS
4 world boxing champions

'When you're as great as I am, it's hard to be humble,' said Muhammad Ali. And when you're as great as he is, it's only right that you should make more money than any other boxer and also be the only man to regain the world heavyweight title twice.

Ali, Muhammad	**Dearfield 3661710**
Foreman, George	**Hayward 5385458**
Frazier, Joe	**Philadelphia 732213**
Norton, Ken	**New York 6864231**

HELP!
12 sources of aid and comfort

Help comes in all shapes and forms. The French novelist, Alexandre Dumas, complained to his doctor that he couldn't sleep. The doctor diagnosed insomnia and prescribed a novel treatment. He told his patient to eat an apple under the Arc de Triomphe every morning at 7.00 A.M. Dumas started sleeping better soon after that. Not everyone shares the same problem, though, and for those who have other anxieties or concerns, the following may be of assistance . . .

Air & Sea Rescue	**Bahamas 23877**
American Atheist Center	**Austin 4581244**
Bible Readings for Today	**Sydney 5693000**
Dial-a-Joke	**New York 9993838**
Dial-a-Prayer	**Sydney 7471555**
Dial Gospel Good News	**Sydney 7471133**

Epilepsy Foundation of America	**Washington DC 2932390**
Gentle Ghost	**London 6039432**
Life-Line	**Sydney 334141**
People Who Care	**Sydney 7132000**
Samaritans	**London 6268654**
Wiesenthal, Simon	**Vienna 639131**

HOLY ORDERS
7 religious sects

There's something to be said for being top dog in a religious order. Until 1773 popes used to have their toes kissed, and the Mormon leader Brigham Young had twenty-seven wives, four of whom he married on one day. The chances of you or I reaching one of these plum posts are pretty slim. It's much safer to start your own sect and for a few guidelines, where better to look than . . .

Albanian Orthodox Diocese of America	**Jamaica Plains 5240477**
Fire Baptized Holiness Church	**Independence 3313049**
Independent Assemblies of God	**San Diego 2951028**
International Church of the Foursquare Gospel	**Los Angeles 4841100**
Israelite House of David	**Benton Harbor 9266695**
Jehovah's Witnesses (US)	**New York 6251240**
Seventh Day Adventists	**Washington DC 7230800**

HOME BASE
a dozen big-league baseball teams

'It took me seventeen years to make three thousand hits in baseball,' admitted American player Hank Aaron. 'I did it in one afternoon on the golf course.' Anyone interested in learning more about this rather over-elaborate version of rounders would be well advised to go straight to the top, to . . .

Baltimore Orioles	**Baltimore 2439800**
Boston Red Sox	**Boston 2679440**
Chicago White Sox	**Chicago 9241000**
Cleveland Indians	**Cleveland 8611200**
Kansas City Royals	**Kansas City 9218000**
Milwaukee Brewers	**Milwaukee 9331818**
Minnesota Twins	**Minnesota 8544040**
New York Yankees	**New York 2934300**
Philadelphia Phillies	**Philadelphia 4636000**
St Louis Cardinals	**St Louis 4213060**
San Diego Padres	**San Diego 2834494**
Texas Rangers	**Arlington 2735223**

HOT FROM THE PRESS
30 of the world's newspapers

If, like many readers, you frequently agree with Adlai Stevenson that, 'Newspaper editors are men who separate the wheat from the chaff, and then print the chaff', there are times when a letter to the editor isn't enough. Under these circumstances a direct call is both more satisfying and more cost-effective. So, here, for the benefit of all would-be complainants, are a few to be getting on with.

Al Ahram	Cairo 59010
Chicago Tribune	Chicago 2223232
Daily Express	London 3538000
Daily Globe	Dodge City 2254151
Daily Mail	London 3536000
Daily News	Dar-es-Salaam 29881
Daily Star	Manchester 2362112
Daily Telegraph	London 3534242
East African Standard	Nairobi 55563
Financial Times	London 2488000
Guardian, The	Manchester 8327200
Herald	Melbourne 630211
Hindustan Times	New Delhi 387707
Illustrated Weekly of India	Bombay 268271
Irish Times	Dublin 722022
La Stampa	Milan 8596
Los Angeles Times	Los Angeles 6252345
Mail	Madras 83931
National Herald	New Delhi 271547
News of the World	London 3533030
New York Times	New York 5561234
Observer, The	London 2360202
Rand Daily Mail	Johannesburg 281500
Scotsman	Edinburgh 2252468
Statesman, The	Calcutta 235361
Sydney Morning Herald	Sydney 4045812
Times, The	London 8371234
Voice of Uganda	Kampala 34403
Washington Post	Washington DC 2236000
Wellington Evening Post	Wellington 729009

INFORMATION I'M REQUESTING ON A SUBJECT INTERESTING . . .
half-a-century of information codes

Anyone charged with the job of giving information down the telephone soon develops a talent for the use of words. Witness one operator, harangued by one abusive caller about the charge he was asked to pay for a long-distance call, answering his, 'I could phone Hell for less than that,' with, 'Yes, sir, that would be a local call.' For information round the world, dial . . .

Addis Ababa **447470**
Amsterdam **66444**
Athens **3222545**
Auckland **260210**
Bangkok **219151**
Beirut **340940**
Belgrade **27**
Berlin **118**
Bogota **810510**
Brussels **130750**
Bucharest **163346**
Buenos Aires **6200156**
Cairo **923000**
Caracas **723881**
Chicago **18002553059**
Copenhagen **111415**
Dublin **47733**
Düsseldorf **118**
Frankfurt **118**
Geneva **323605**

Hamburg **118**
Helsinki **1623217**
Hong Kong **367111**
Istanbul **406864**
Karachi **510234**
Kuala Lumpur **0380778**
Lima **38440**
Lisbon **367031**
London **6299191**
Los Angeles **18002553059**
Manila **482231**
Mexico City **5853060**
Moscow **2922692**
Munich **118**
Nairobi **23265**
Nassau **916**
New York **18002553059**
Oslo **427170**
Paris **7201678**
Rio de Janeiro **2366609**

San Juan **7911054**   Tel Aviv **223266**
Singapore **633611**   Tokyo **2161901**
Stockholm **221840**   Vienna **579657**
Sydney **013**   Washington **18002553059**
Taipei **544537**   Zurich **256700**

IN THE NET
11 football teams

If, as Howard Cosell contends, 'Sport is the toy department of
human life', the arrival of ever more violent children's
amusements goes a long way to explaining the violence on the
terraces. Anyone with ideas on how to sort out the problem
could approach these for starters . . .

Arsenal   **London 2260304**
Celtic   **Glasgow 5542710**
Fort Lauderdale Strikers   **Fort Lauderdale 4915140**
Las Vegas Quicksilvers   **Las Vegas 7338326**
Liverpool   **Liverpool 2632361**
Manchester United   **Manchester 8721661**
Rangers   **Glasgow 4270159**
Tampa Bay Rowdies   **Tampa 8701122**
Vancouver Whitecaps   **Vancouver 6832255**
Waneroo Football Club   **Perth 4099548**
Yugal Prague Soccer Club   **Sydney 6613580**

I SPY
7 manufacturers of photographic equipment

There was once a Hollywood movie with the title *I am a Camera* which received one masterly review, 'Me no Leica'. That brand name has been a bit eclipsed by those from the land of the rising sun, which explains why most of the numbers you're likely to need come from Japan.

Agfa-Gevaert	**Morstel-Antwerp 401940**
Asahi Optical Co	**Tokyo 7582111**
Eastman Kodak	**Rochester 3252000**
Minolta	**Osaka 2712251**
Olympus	**Tokyo 3772111**
Ricoh	**Tokyo 7728111**
Yashica	**Tokyo 4001411**

LATEST, LATEST, READ ALL ABOUT IT
15 worldwide news agencies

Newspapermen, if you ask them, take differing attitudes towards their profession. Ben Bradlee, editor of the *Washington Post*, saw news as 'the first rough draft of history', whereas Evelyn Waugh, in *Scoop*, gave a different interpretation, 'News is what a chap who doesn't care much about anything wants to read. And it's only news until he's read it. After that it's dead.' Dead or alive news still manages to keep one half of the world guessing while the other half is making it, and to

keep abreast of the latest developments you can't beat your own hot line to the world's agencies.

Agence-France Presse	**Paris 4540**
Associated Press	**London 3531515**
Australian Associated Press	**Sydney 293941**
Bar-David	**Tel Aviv 751048**
Bermuda News Bureau	**Hamilton 11221**
Central News Agency	**Taipei 550379**
Free Information Bureau	**New York 8763688**
Futures Information Network	**New York 6610884**
News Reports	**Melbourne 6205**
Packaged Facts	**New York 5325533**
Religious News Service	**New York 6887094**
Reuters	**London 3535200**
Tass	**Moscow 2297225**
Western Union FYI News Service	**Upper Saddle River 8255103**
World Wide Information Services	**New York 6767240**

MATCH-MAKING
6 ways to find the perfect partner

With divorce almost as rampant as inflation it's a wonder that people still bother to try and establish life-long relationships, and there are plenty of advisers around to tell you that the institution isn't all it's cracked up to be. Here's Helen Rowland, for one: 'When a girl marries, she exchanges the attentions of many men for the inattention of one'; or Zsa Zsa

Gabor, who's had more experience than most: 'A man is never complete until he's married. Then he's finished.' All the same there are still many willing souls happy to give it a try, some through groups like . . .

Comdates Computing Services	**San Francisco 3918181**
Compu-Dating Service	**New York 2794358**
Dateline	**London 9376503**
Matchmaker	**London 7301542**
Phone-a-friend	**Sydney 6600061**
Sappho	**London 7243636**

MEDITATION MEDIUM
half-a-dozen yoga centres

Ananda Yoga Sivanda	**London 3887745**
Breathing and Health Seminars with Sarama Hare Krishna Bhakti	**New York 5231430**
Ho Foundation	**Toronto 9640612**
International Society for Krishna Consciousness	**Dublin 743767**
Lotus Health and Beauty Centre	**Randburg 6788813**
Yoga Retreat	**Auckland 4128075**

THE MEDIUM IS THE MASSAGE
or a touch of class

Callers on Johannesburg 238146 receive the answer 'Brian Marks', which can prove more than a little disconcerting for those in search of a gentle, relaxing rub-down. First impressions are so important, particularly in this business.

Bikini Girls Massage & Sauna	**Perth 3612317**
Bodyguard Massage Studios	**Dublin 963327**
Bondi Junction Health Centre	**Sydney 3895072**
Brian Marks Health Centre	**Johannesburg 238146**
Edith Szasz Therapeutical & Connective Tissue Massage	**Toronto 9228169**
Mademoiselle de Massage	**New York 7594565**
Magic Touch Massage	**London 7485569**
Michelle's Special	**San Francisco 6618224**

MINE WORKINGS
20 sources of metals and minerals from around the world and deep inside it

There's a Texan mining company listed below which comes in for more than its fair share of cranky phone calls. Switchboard operators answer, quite rightly, 'Sunshine Mining' and get such replies as, 'Why are you working in the dark then?' Some people never see the light.

Alcanaluminum	**Montreal 8772340**
Amax	**Greenwich 6223000**
Ashanti Goldfields	**Accra 2036**
Bethlehem Copper	**Ashcroft 575424**
BHP	**Melbourne 4990621**
Borg Mining	**Monrovia 22155**
Bunker Hill	**Kellogg 7841261**
Charbonnage de France	**Paris 2259500**
Consolidated Goldfields	**London 6061020**
Consolidated Goldfields, Australia	**Sydney 20512**
Falconbridge Nickel Mines	**Toronto 8637000**
Gold Fields of South Africa	**Johannesburg 8388381**
Homestake Mining	**San Francisco 9818150**
Jordan Phosphate Mines	**Amman 38147**
Mogul of Ireland	**Dublin 760901**
Rio Tinto-Zinc	**London 9302399**
Rossing Uranium	**Johannesburg 8381641**
Sunshine Mining	**Dallas 7489872**
3M	**St Paul 7331110**
Western Collieries	**Perth 3252711**

MONEY MATTERS
a dozen finance ministries

We shouldn't be fooled by the men who hold the world's purse strings. Grand and imposing they may sound when rambling on about economics, but when it comes down to the nitty gritty, they're as fallible as the rest of us. 'I often wondered what those damned dots meant,' said Sir Winston Churchill's father, Lord Randolph, referring to decimal points, and he'd been Chancellor of the Exchequer by that time! There's no need to feel abashed, therefore, if you don't fully understand what's going on with the world's finances. Just get on the blower and demand an explanation. It'll be amusing to see if anyone else is any the wiser . . .

Belgium	**Brussels 5131920**
Cyprus	**Nicosia 70213**
Denmark	**Copenhagen 111141**
France	**Paris 2336633**
Germany, West	**Bonn 886645**
Ireland	**Dublin 767571**
Italy	**Rome 5997**
Jordan	**Amman 39310**
Luxembourg	**Luxembourg 478215**
Netherlands	**The Hague 767767**
Portugal	**Lisbon 321909**
United Kingdom	**London 2333000**

MOTOR SHOW
Two dozen of the world's leading car manufacturers

At today's prices a Rolls-Royce will set you back as much as £83,000, though armour plating comes a little dearer. Kiss goodbye to £170,000 if you want all-round bullet-proof protection. All in all, a few discreet enquiries could save a lot of embarrassment later. Of course your reason for giving the manufacturer a call might be totally different. With not far short of 160,000,000 cars on America's roads alone, there must be getting on for that many motorists who at some time in their lives feel like screaming down the phone to let off a little steam when their vehicles pack up. Better by far to go straight to the man at the top. For the price of a phone call, some not so far from home, the results can be most rewarding!

Alfa Romeo	**Milan 3977**
American Motors	**Southfield 8271000**
BMW	**Munich 38951**
British Leyland	**London 4866000**
Chrysler	**Detroit 9565252**
DAF	**Eindhoven 149111**
Daihatsu	**Osaka 518811**
Daimler-Benz	**Stuttgart 3021**
FIAT	**Turin 65651**
Ford	**Dearborn 3223000**
Fuji Heavy Industries	**Tokyo 3472340**
General Motors	**Detroit 5565000**
Hino	**Tokyo 833111**
Honda	**Tokyo 4990111**
Isuzu	**Tokyo 7621111**
Nissan	**Tokyo 5435523**
Peugeot-Citroën	**Paris 2672000**
Renault	**Billancourt 6031313**
Rolls-Royce	**London 8397888**
Saab-Scania Aktiebolag	**Linköping 4613115400**
Suzuki	**Shizuoka 471111**
Toyota	**Aichi 282121**
Volkswagen	**Wolfsburg 05361/221**
Volvo	**Gothenburg 590000**

NET CALL
5 tennis champions

Among the high-earning élite of the international tennis circuit Jimmy Connors still holds the record for the highest prize from one match, a challenge match in 1975 in which he beat John Newcombe and collected half a million dollars.

Ashe, Arthur	**Washington DC 2962146**
Connors, Jimmy	**Belleville 3983313**
King, Billie Jean	**San Mateo 5744622**
Lloyd, Chris	**San Francisco 6732018**
Smith, Stan	**Washington DC 6712599**

NIGHT-LIFE
25 nightspots from Baghdad to Taipei

'Seems like the only place on a wet night,' said one night club customer to a waiter as he booked a table for later in the evening by phone. 'Sure is,' said the waiter. 'Stay outside and get wet or come in and get soaked.' If you should ever be caught in a similar dilemma it's possible that one of the following may provide a haven.

Balada	**Bucharest 140400**
Bal de Moulin Rouge	**Paris 6060019**
Beauty Palace	**Taipei 5550351**
La Belle Epoque	**Sharjah 356557**
Blow-up	**Caracas 335086**
Blue Dolphin	**Honolulu 9230711**

Bocaccio	**Johannesburg 2473136**
Bonanza	**Oslo 334870**
El Castellano	**Manila 894011**
Le Chat Noir	**Melbourne 5090277**
Drink	**Rio de Janeiro 2577068**
Embassy	**London 4995974**
Ewan Super Night Club	**Abu Dhabi 41184**
Les Girls	**Sydney 3582333**
Hotel Imperial	**New Delhi 311511**
Maverick's Flat	**Los Angeles 2954179**
Moulin Rouge	**Baghdad 90809**
Oasis	**Karachi 511056**
Pub Manço	**Istanbul 466059**

Purple Onion	**San Francisco 7810835**
Red Baron	**San Juan 7255234**
Le Sexy	**Paris 2252517**
Starlight Supper Club	**Kuwait 530000**
Sunset Club	**Lima 229874**
Tradewinds	**Singapore 372233**

NOVEL NUMBERS
25 world novelists and their agents

Alistair MacLean is the only novelist to have written eighteen
novels which have each sold over a million copies. Sadly not
every author is as successful, as Jules Renard remarked,
'Writing is the only profession where no one considers you
ridiculous if you earn no money', though few of those
mentioned here are exactly on the breadline.

Asimov, Isaac	**New York 3621564**
Braine, John	**Woking 67014**
Buckley, William	**New York OR 97330**
Clarke, Arthur C.	**Colombo 94255**
Dahl, Roald	**Great Missenden 2757**
Deighton, Len	**London 6369395**
Dickens, Monica	**Boston 5633225**
Du Maurier, Daphne	**Par 2706**
Fowles, John	**London 6362901**
Greene, Graham	**London 8369081**
Haley, Alex	**Washington DC 6380348**
Hammond Innes, Ralph	**Hadleigh 3294**
Lee, Laurie	**London 3522197**
MacLean, Alistair	**London 4937070**
Mailer, Norman	**New York 2455500**
Naipaul, V. S.	**London 5802746**

Paço d'Arcos, Joquim	**Lisbon 43325**
Powell, Anthony	**Frome 84314**
Simenon, Georges	**Lausanne 333979**
Solzhenitsyn, Alexander	**New York 5937000**
Spark, Muriel	**London 8366633**
Updike, John	**New York 7512600**
Uris, Leon	**New York 9534561**
Vidal, Gore	**New York JU65100**
Vonnegut, Kurt Jr	**New York 6887008**

ON THE BEAT
the world's police

There is a school of thought which holds that crime doesn't pay; however, a quick look at some of the statistics shows that this isn't universally true. The Chicago police, for instance, have met with disappointment in a number of fields. Only thirteen convictions have been made from over 1,000 murders committed in the city in the last seventy-odd years. That's why the police need all the help they can get and that's why any responsible citizen should know how to call them wherever he or she may be.

Addis Ababa **01**	Geneva **117**
Amsterdam **222222**	Glasgow **999**
Athens **100**	Hamburg **110**
Auckland **111**	Helsinki **002**
Bangkok **810818**	Hong Kong **002**
Barcelona **091**	Istanbul **274500**
Beirut **16**	Johannesburg **30**
Belgrade **92**	Karachi **222222**
Berlin **110**	Kuala Lumpur **0**
Bogota **12**	Lisbon **366141**
Brussels **906**	London **999**
Buenos Aires **101**	Los Angeles **0**
Cairo **912644**	Madrid **091**
Caracas **111**	Manila **717**
Chicago **0**	Melbourne **000**
Copenhagen **000**	Milan **113**
Dublin **999**	Montreal **8721313**
Düsseldorf **110**	Moscow **02**
Frankfurt **110**	Munich **110**

Nairobi **999**
Nassau **24444**
New York **0**
Oslo **110011**
Paris **17**
Rio de Janeiro **2222121**
Rome **113**
San Juan **3432020**
Singapore **999**
Stockholm **90000**

Sydney **000**
Taipei **169**
Tel Aviv **100**
Tokyo **110**
Toronto **967222**
Vancouver **6652211**
Vienna **123**
Washington DC **0**
Zurich **117**

ON THE WAGON
or 10 ways of helping you climb up

A branch of Alcoholics Anonymous which opened in the
northern Australian city of Darwin had to close soon after
through lack of support. However, those wishing to fight the
bottle in other parts of the world should meet with greater
success through the help of . . .

Alateen   **Perth 3257528**
Alcohol and Drugs
  Problem Association of
  North America   **Washington DC 4520990**
Alcoholics Anonymous   **Brisbane 2217920**
Alcoholics Anonymous   **Dublin 774809**
Alcoholics Anonymous   **London 8348202**
Alcoholics Anonymous
  World Service (Grand
  Central Station)   **New York 6861100**
American Temperance
  Society   **Washington DC 7230800**
City Alcoholic Treatment
  Center   **Chicago 2543680**

| Irish National Council of Alcoholism | **Dublin 774832** |
| Salvation Army Alcohol and Drug Addiction Centre | **Sydney 2722322** |

ON THE WATERFRONT
20 dockyards

Big is the name of the game in shipbuilding today. The world's longest ship, an oil tanker, is the best part of a quarter of a mile long and it's not uncommon for the crews on ships this size to get from one end to the other by bicycle. The industry's going through a rough time at the moment, of course, and any orders are willingly received. If you can use a freighter or two, try . . .

Allied Shipbuilders	**Vancouver 9292365**
American Marine Corp	**New Orleans 2425200**
Bazan	**Madrid 4415100**
Blohm & Voss	**Hamburg 3061**
Brooke Marine	**Lowestoft 65221**
Cantiere Navale Breda	**Venice 59860**
Dillingham Corp	**Sydney 279231**
DTCN	**Paris 2603330**
Evans Deakin Industries	**Brisbane 218338**
Harland & Wolff	**Belfast 58456**
Hellenic Shipyards Co	**Athens 073471**
Hongkong & Wampoa Dock Co	**Kowloon 334111**
Israel Shipyards Ltd	**Haifa 749111**
Maritime Maintenance	**Sydney 291488**
Maryland Shipping & Drydock Co	**Baltimore 3550500**
Neresbu	**The Hague 602813**
Nylands Verksted	**Oslo 410000**
Verolme United Shipyards	**Rotterdam 162500**
Vosper Thornycroft	**Portsmouth 499121**
Yarrow Shipbuilders	**Glasgow 9591207**

OPERATIC NUMBERS
25 of the world's opera houses

Sir Thomas Beecham once had cause to regret the facility of modern communications. Prior to a performance of *Tristan* in a provincial theatre, he informed the manager what scenery would be needed and left the matter at that, having taken the trouble to emphasize the importance of a tower in one act. Without having actually seen the set on the night in question Sir Thomas opened the performance and only when the curtain was raised on the act requiring the tower did he see the set from Act Two of *Iolanthe*, with Big Ben in the background. Those with similar instructions to convey would be well advised to make full use of the telephone and check that all is well before it's too late.

Bavarian State Opera	**Munich 221316**
Colisseum	**London 8363161**
Deutsche Opera	**Berlin 3414449**
Drottingholm Staatsteater	**Stockholm 630510**
Glyndebourne Festival Opera	**Lewes 411**
Grand Opéra	**Bordeaux 485854**
Hamburgische Staatsoper	**Hamburg 351555**
Metropolitan Opera	**New York 7993100**
Opéra	**Lyon 280960**
Opéra	**Paris 0735750**
Opéra de Monte Carlo	**Monte Carlo 306931**
Opéra de Wallonie	**Liège 235910**
Opéra Municipal	**Marseilles 330358**
Opéra Municipal	**Nice 856731**
Operhaus	**Graz 76451**
Richard Wagner Festspielhaus	**Bayreuth 5722**
Royal Opera House, Covent Garden	**London 2401911**
Rudaki Opera Hall	**Tehran 45154**
Sadler's Wells	**London 8371672**
Staatsoper	**Vienna 527636**
Teatro alla Scala	**Milan 8879**
Teatro dell'Opera	**Rome 463641**
Teatro San Carlo	**Naples 390745**
Théâtre Municipal	**Strasbourg 364341**

OWZAT
11 cricketers

While headmaster of Repton, Archbishop William Temple
was once heard to remark, 'Personally, I have always looked
on cricket as organized loafing.' Not everyone would agree
with him on this, least of all . . .

Bedi, Bishan	**Amritsar 43133**
Benaud, Richie	**Sydney 6656464**
Botham, Ian	**Taunton 72946**
Chandrasekhar, Bhagwat	**Jayanagar 41268**
Chappell, Greg	**Kenmore 2295416**
Cowdrey, Colin	**Limpsfield 2838989**
Hutton, Sir Leonard	**Kingston-upon-Thames 9420604**
Laker, Jim	**London 8742133**
Lillie, Dennis	**Perth 3610555**
Lloyd, Clive	**Manchester 8725533**
Willis, Bob	**Birmingham 4404292**

PALACE CONNECTIONS
16 royal residences and other palaces

Either through an oversight or a misplaced sense of economy, the enormous palace of the French monarchs was built at Versailles without a single lavatory being incorporated in the design. To avoid the obvious complications this involves, prospective royal visitors are advised to confirm the existence of the necessary facilities in advance by phoning . . .

Amir's Palace	**Doha 25241**
Blenheim Palace	**Woodstock 811325**
Buckingham Palace	**London 9304832**
Château-de-Versailles	**Versailles 9505832**
Golestan Palace	**Tehran 532257**
Guest Palace	**Bahrain 712821**
Hammersmith Palais de Danse	**London 7482812**
Lambeth Palace	**London 9286222**
Palais de Fontainebleau	**Fontainebleau 4222740**
Palazzo de Venezia	**Rome 6798865**
Palazzo Ducale	**Venice 24951**
Palazzo Pitti	**Florence 23440**
Palazzo Vecchio	**Florence 27681**
Royal Palace	**Oslo 441920**
Scone Palace	**Scone 51416**
Topkapi Palace	**Istanbul 283547**

PARTY LINES
a dozen political groupings

Robert Louis Stevenson thought that 'Politics is perhaps the only profession for which no preparation is thought necessary,' so if you've a mind to try your hand at a new career, you might consider contacting . . .

Black Panther Party	**Oakland 6380195**
Central Committee of the Communist Party of the Soviet Union	**Moscow 2062511**
Communist Party	**New York 9894994**
Conservative & Unionist Party	**London 2229000**
Democratic National Committee	**Washington DC 7975900**
Fine Gael	**Dublin 761573**
Labour Party	**London 8349434**
National Socialist White People's Party (formerly American Nazi Party)	**Arlington 5242175**
Republican National Committee	**Washington DC 4846500**
Republican People's Party	**Ankara 283120**
Sinn Fein	**Dublin 781552**
Tamil United Liberation Front	**Jaffna 7176**

PEAK CALLS
a dozen mountains to help you get away from it all

Yes, even mountains haven't escaped the influx of the telephone. That's to say there are a good few listed in the

world's directories, though inevitably most of them are in North America. If you fancy dialling the third on the list, you might be well advised to do so in private and preferably without the aid of the operator. Trying to explain you want to dial a mountain called Loon, might be more trouble than it's worth.

Big Mountain	**Whitefish 8623511**
Crystal Mountain	**Thompsonville 4386000**
Loon Mountain	**Lincoln 7458111**
Mammoth Mountain	**Mammoth Lakes 9342571**
Mont Alyeska	**Girdwood 7836000**
Mont Tremblant	**Sutton 8616165**
Mount Norquay	**Banff 2616574**
Mount Seymour	**Vancouver 9883326**

Mount Snow	**West Dover 4643333**
Spirit Mountain	**Duluth 6282891**
Squaw Mountain	**Greenville 6952272**
West Mountain	**Glen Falls 7936606**

PHONE FORECASTING
25 weather reports

There are some freak weather conditions that can never be predicted, like the snowfall in the middle of the Sahara which stopped traffic in Algeria in February 1979. But on the whole modern weather forecasting is pretty accurate and a call to any of the following should give you an idea of what's in store.

Amsterdam **003**	Melbourne **6064**
Berlin **1164**	Milan **7390**
Brussels **991**	Munich **1164**
Bucharest **05**	Nassau **915**
Buenos Aires **324480**	Paris **7054070**
Caracas **410279**	Rome **59061**
Dublin **1199**	San Juan **7910320**
Frankfurt **1164**	Stockholm **239500**
Geneva **162**	Sydney **2071**
Glasgow **2468091**	Taipei **166**
Hamburg **1164**	Vienna **1566**
Helsinki **038**	Zurich **162**
London **2468091**	

PLAYING THE GAME
12 sports bodies

According to Sir Herbert Beerbohm Tree, 'The national sport of England is obstacle racing. People fill their rooms with useless and cumbersome furniture, and spend the rest of their lives in trying to dodge it.' More obvious activities take place too, and to keep abreast of the latest developments in these the following organizations should be of help.

American Racing Drivers' Club	**Bristol 7880776**
Cricket Club of India	**Bombay 291019**
Golden Gloves Association of America	**Albuquerque 2989286**
International Cyclists' Union	**Geneva 263611**
International Golf Association	**New York 5812220**
International Olympic Committee	**Lausanne 253271**
International Tennis Federation	**London 3858441**
Mountaineering Federation	**Tehran 822053**
NSW Cricket Association	**Sydney 274053**
Rodeo News Bureau	**Denver 4553270**
World Boxing Council	**Mexico City 5691911**
World Team Tennis Inc	**St Louis 7277211**

THE PLAY'S THE THING
25 playwrights and their agents

Agatha Christie takes first prize for the longest non-stop run with *The Mousetrap* which has been playing for thirty years and has passed its 12,500th performance. Then, of course, there are those shows which never even see a second night, like *Frankenstein* which opened and closed on Broadway in the same evening in 1981 with a loss of something in the region of $2 million. As William Saroyan observed, 'You write a hit play the same way you write a flop.'

Albee, Edward	**New York 5865100**
Arrabal, Fernando	**Paris 5226894**
Ayckbourn, Alan	**London 2400691**
Beckett, Samuel	**Paris 2223794**
Bolt, Robert	**London 8367403**
Bond, Edward	**London 2400691**
Buero Vallejo, Antonia	**Madrid 4025614**
Hampton, Christopher	**London 2292188**
Havel, Václav	**Prague 3299592**
Hockwälder, Fritz	**Zurich 532073**
Miller, Arthur	**New York 4905700**
Osborne, John	**London 7347311**
Pinter, Harold	**London 2352797**
Porter, Hal	**Garroc 918201**
Rabe, David	**New York 6631582**
Rózécwicz, Taduesz	**Wroclaw 64338**
Shaffer, Peter	**London 6026892**
Simon, Neil	**Beverly Hills 2785692**
Simpson, Norman	**London 5800604**
Stoppard, Tom	**London 7347311**
Storey, David	**London 6369395**
Terzakis, Anghelos	**Syndesmona 3618223**
Ustinov, Peter	**London 7349361**
Wesker, Arnold	**London 3405125**
Weyraveh, Wolfgang	**Darmstadt 46759**

POETS' CORNER
20 world poets and their agents

'Poets,' said Wilson Mizner, 'are born, not paid.' To confirm both facts contact . . .

Aliger, Margarita	**Moscow 2315894**
Betjeman, John	**London 4934361**
Birney, Earle	**Toronto 4898368**
Bordier, Roger	**Paris 5352256**
Bottrall, Francis	**Rome 489989**
Butler, Frederick	**Grahamstown (South Africa) 3823**
Dickey, James	**Columbia 7879962**
Eberhart, Richard	**Hanover 6432938**
Elytis, Odysseus	**Athens 3626458**
Gibbons, Stella	**London 3402566**
Ginsberg, Allen	**San Francisco 3628193**
Graves, Robert	**London 4051057**
Holan, Vladimir	**Prague 532377**
Holub, Miroslav	**Prague 4123602**
Hughes, Ted	**London 2786881**
Narovchatov, Sergey	**Moscow 1303458**
Pant, Sumitranadan	**Allahabad 3540**
Pitter, Ruth	**Long Crendon 208373**
Seiffert, Jaroslav	**Prague 357871**
Varnai, Zseni	**Budapest 361346**

PRESIDENTS
6 men at the top

According to Richard Nixon he would have made a good Pope. Gerald Ford wanted to take the entire nation into the locker room to give them a pep-talk at half-time. And Barry Goldwater summed up the presidency like this: 'I would not be truthful if I said I was fully qualified for the office. I do not play the piano, I seldom play golf, and I never play touch football.' For anyone who still has faith in democracy and its alternatives, these gentlemen may be glad to hear from you.

Andropov, Yuri	**Moscow 2062511**
Hilary, Patrick	**Dublin 772815**
Mitterrand, François	**Paris 2615100**
Reagan, Ronald	**Washington DC 4562573**
Pertini, Alessandro	**Rome 4699**
Scheel, Walter	**Bonn 2001**

PRIVATE EYES
12 sleuths to snoop and spy

A young man rang Pinkerton's one morning and said he wanted to join their team. He didn't have any experience as a detective, he confessed, but he was willing to learn. 'I see,' said the voice on the other end of the line, 'you want to be a private pupil.' The young man didn't get the joke, or the job.

Bow Street Investigation Services	**London 8529788**
Burns International Security Services	**New York 7621000**
Cape Investigation Bureau	**Cape Town 455826**
Hopkinson Investigation Services	**Toronto 3635858**
King's Investigation Services	**London 4050343**
McRoberts Agency	**New York 9445393**

Metropolitan International	New York 7650560
Monte's Investigation	Sydney 274800
Pat Kohn Detective	
Agency	San Francisco 7514554
Pinkerton's	New York 2854860
Prevention and Detection	London 2427112
Special Investigation	
Bureau	Dublin 978015

PROBLEM SOLVERS
18 helping hands

'Problems,' said some sage, 'are only opportunities in work clothes', but when you haven't anything else to change into, to continue the metaphor, you soon get tired of the wardrobe. In circumstances like this you may need . . .

Analytical Psychology of Ontario	**Toronto 9619767**
Association for Voluntary Sterilization	**New York 9863880**
Bible Answers to Life's Problems	**Sydney 5691000**
Catholic Marriage Advisory Council	**London 7270141**
Committee for the Scientific Investigation of Claims of the Paranormal	**Buffalo 8370306**
Euthanasia Education Council	**New York 2466962**
Gamblers Anonymous	**Los Angeles 3868789**
The Haven Drug Centre	**Brisbane 3972292**
Hypnosis Centre	**Sydney 9775149**
Iran-American Society	**Tehran 640501**
Iran Soviet Cultural Society	**Tehran 651239**
National Sex Forum	**San Francisco 9281133**
Problem Limited	**London 8288181**
Release	**London 6039432**
Sichering (oral contraceptives and fertility pills)	**Berlin 468**
Soul Talk	**Sydney 7476311**

Venereal Disease Info	**Sydney 0513**
Wayside Chapel Crisis	
Centre	**Sydney 334151**

PRODUCTION NUMBERS
30 producers and directors and their agents

On the subject of theatre directors Rhetta Hughes had this to
say: 'There are two kinds of directors in the theatre. Those
who think they are God and those who are certain of it.' No
doubt others have aired similar feelings about film directors.
For first-hand experience why not go straight to the people in
question?

Altman, Robert	**Los Angeles 4754987**
Axer, Erwin	**Warsaw 440116**
Barton, John	**Bidford-on-Avon 2275**
Bondarchuk, Sergey	**Moscow 2292795**
Boorman, John	**Wicklow 5177**
Boulting, Roy	**London 3526838**
Bradini, Aleksander	**Warsaw 252122**
Cacoyannis, Michael	**Athens 9922054**
Carné, Marcel	**Paris 5240178**
Chabrol, Claude	**Neuilly-sur-Seine (Maillot) 8849**
Coppola, Francis Ford	**San Francisco 4210151**
De Laurentis, Dino	**Rome 5915551**
Demy, Jacques	**Paris 3226600**
Dexter, John	**New York 7993100**
Donner, Jörn	**Helsinki 652675**
Fábri, Zoltán	**Budapest 116650**
Fleckstein, Günther	**Göttingham-Geismar 59471**

Grotowski, Jerzy	**Wroclaw 34267**
Hands, Terry	**Stratford-upon-Avon 3693**
Inagaki, Hiroshi	**Tokyo 4830845**
Ivory, James	**New York 5828049**
Koun, Karolos	**Athens 3228706**
Losey, Joseph	**Paris 3252759**
Nunn, Trevor	**Stratford-upon-Avon 3693**
Prince, Harold	**New York 3990960**
Ray, Satyajit	**Calcutta 448747**
Schlesinger, John	**London 7347421**
Truffaut, François	**Paris 25612734**
Winner, Michael	**London 7348385**
Zinneman, Fred	**London 4998810**

RADIAL PATTERN
9 rubber companies

Believe it or not, rubber is used to make bubble gum. If it
wasn't for the rubber, the bubbles would be far more difficult,
not to say impossible, to blow. Rubber is used for other
purposes too and to find out which, the following should be of
help . . .

Bridgestone	**Tokyo 5670111**
Dunlop Australia	**Melbourne 630371**
Dunlop Holdings	**London 9306700**
Firestone	**Akron 3797000**
Goodrich, B.F.	**Akron 3792000**
Goodyear	**Akron 7942121**
Michelin	**Clermont-Ferrand 924195**
Pirelli	**Milan 62221**
Uniroyal	**New York 4894000**

RENDEZ-VOUS
20 meeting points to see and be seen at

Dial Johannesburg 8341345 for Rendez-vous and you're
likely to get more than you bargained for, though you're not
likely to complain. That particular Rendez-vous runs an
escort agency. The ones below may prove equally rewarding,
but there your liaisons are nothing to do with the
management.

Arthur's	**Sydney 3585097**
Blow-up	**Hong Kong 297775**
Bottoms Up	**Atlanta 8751043**
The Cat's Den	**Montreal 9324584**
Chez Toi	**Tehran 894371**
Club 58	**Geneva 354500**
Dreams House	**Rawalpindi 68488**
Gay Gordon	**Glasgow 2483040**
Grand Bazaar	**Istanbul 270004**
Horse Shoe	**Karachi 411439**
Le New Jimmy's	**Paris 3267414**
Mau-Mau	**Buenos Aires 416853**
Maxim	**Shiraz 37598**
Penthouse Club	**Copenhagen 143535**
People's Assembly	**Cairo 49988**
Piper Club	**Rome 854439**
River Club	**London 8341621**
Sea Club	**Brussels 2182534**
Trade Winds Lounge	**. Nassau 55441**
Walnut Tree	**Melbourne 3284409**

ROCK AND FOLK
12 of the world's stars and their agents

Engelbert Humperdinck holds the record (if you'll pardon
the expression) for the longest uninterrupted stretch at the top
of the British hit parade and Cliff Richard has been there
more often than any other British singer. The others haven't
done so badly either.

Baez, Joan	**Menlo Park 3280266**
Diamond, Neil	**Los Angeles 5507100**
Dylan, Bob	**New York 6916820**
Essex, David	**London 5890884**

Humperdinck, Engelbert	**London 6299255**
Jagger, Mick	**New York 3622700**
John, Elton	**London 4912777**
Manilow, Barry	**New York 5954330**
Midler, Bette	**New York 4867100**
Newton-John, Olivia	**Los Angeles 5504000**
Richard, Cliff	**London 4864182**
Ross, Diana	**Los Angeles 4683491**

ROOM NUMBERS
**top-class accommodation in 30 of the world's major
hotels**

If you're reckoning on spending a few nights in Moscow and
are worried that you might be a bit lonely, you should check
in to the Rossiya. With a staff of 3,000 and accommodation for
twice that number, there's no risk of you being without
company. For something a little more spacious, the Waldorf
Astoria may be more to your liking. It covers an entire block
of New York City measuring over one and three-quarter
acres, and has forty-seven storeys. You'll find the rest a bit less
daunting.

Amir	**Mashad 21300**
Beach Luxury	**Karachi 551031**
Bristol	**Sarajevo 614811**
Caesar's Palace	**Las Vegas 7317110**
Canberra	**Cannes 382070**
Claridges	**London 6298860**
Coconut Grove	**Miami 4433812**
Continental	**Luanda 25231**
El Cid	**Caracas 339761**
Faletti's	**Lahore 53861**

Flashman's	**Rawalpindi 64811**
Gazebo	**Brisbane 2216177**
George V	**Paris 7235400**
Grand	**N'Djamena 3888**
Hilton	**Chicago 3411770**
Holiday Inn	**Memphis 3624001**
Horon	**Trebizond 1199**
Hotel of Nationalities	**Peking 668541**
Intercontinental	**Managua 23530**
International Atahualpa	**Guayaquil 306800**
La Reserve	**Geneva 741741**
Persepolis Inn	**Persepolis 21052**
Raffles	**Singapore 328041**
Ritz	**Paris 2603830**
Rossiya	**Moscow 2985400**
Savoy	**London 8364343**
Slavija	**Belgrade 450842**
Waldorf Astoria	**New York 3553000**
Watergate	**Washington DC 9652300**
Wentworth	**Sydney 2300700**

ROYAL PROGRESS
10 of the world's crowned heads

King Sobhuza II of Swaziland is the world's longest reigning
monarch at the time of writing, coming to the throne when he
was four months old in December 1899. To find out what
things were like then, you can ring him on Kwaluseni 50. As
for the rest, ring on . . .

Amir of Bahrain	**Bahrain 66451**
Amir of Qatar	**Doha 25241**
Asantahene	**Kumasi 3680**

King Olav	**Oslo 441920**
King Sobhuza II	**Kwaluseni 50**
Prince Abdul Rahman	**Penang 65970**
Prince Dlamini	**Mbabane 2251**
Queen Elizabeth II	**London 9304832**
Raja of Perlis	**Perlis 7552211**
Sultan of Johore	**Johore JB 2000**

SEATS OF GOVERNMENT
governments totalitarian, democratic and chaotic

It's generally held that only one man had the right idea about governments – and he was Guy Fawkes. Still, if 'government of the people, by the people, and for the people' really does exist, these numbers may come in handy the next time red tape threatens to strangle you.

Capitol (Doorkeeper)	**Washington DC 2253505**
Central Committee, Communist Party	**Moscow 2062511**
Chancellery	**Bonn 56**
Council of Ministers	**Bahrain 253361**
Council of Ministers	**Sofia 8691**
Council of State	**Warsaw 287001**
Dail Eireann	**Dublin 789911**
Dept of Cabinet Affairs	**Dubai 431036**
Government	**Sharjah 354501**
House of Councillors	**Tokyo 5813111**
House of Representatives	**Tokyo 5815111**
House of Representatives	**Washington DC 2243121**
Houses of Parliament	**London 2193000**
Ministry of State	**Ankara 128400**
Parliament	**Ankara 176966**
Presidential Court	**Abu Dhabi 41010**
Presidency of the Cabinet	**Rome 6779**
Presidency of Government	**Madrid 4190300**
Regierung	**Vienna 635631**
Ruler's Majilis	**Fujairah 22333**
Ruler's Office	**Ajman 22248**
Ruler's Office	**Uum al-Quainwain 66125**

Seanad Eireann	**Dublin 789771**
Secretaryship of the Presidium	**Budapest 321750**
Secretaryship of State	**Luxembourg 4781**
Senate	**Amman 22110**
Senate	**Washington DC 2243121**

SHOPPER'S GUIDE
50 of the world's top shops

It's not unknown for customers to ring a major chain of British chemists in the mistaken belief that they will find footwear and Safeways get the odd call too from customers anxious about home security. Phone calls are expensive, especially if you dial Gucci in error. They can be frustrating too. So to save time and effort (if not money) we've whittled world shopping down to a manageable size.

Åhlen & Holm	**Stockholm 449000**
Ahold	**Zaandam 599111**
Au Printemps	**Paris 2852222**
Bager Mohebi Stores	**Abu Dhabi 41417**
Bager Mohebi Stores	**Ras al-Khaimah 21358**
Bay Department Stores	**Toronto 9645511**
Boans	**Perth 230121**
Bon Marché	**Seattle 6241234**
Boots	**Nottingham 56111**
Carrefour	**Courcouronnes 0779240**
Consumer Buying Corp-oration	**Ndola 2681**
David Jones	**Sydney 20664**

134

Debenhams	**London** 5804444
Food Fair Stores	**Philadelphia** 3829500
Fortnum & Mason	**London** 7348040
Galeries Lafayette	**Paris** 2823456
Grands Magasins Jelmoli	**Zurich** 29301
Grand Magazzini Coin	**Mexico City** 53200
Gucci	**Los Angeles** 2783451
Harrods	**London** 7301234
Heacock	**Manila** 595823
Horten	**Düsseldorf** 59901
House of Fraser	**Glasgow** 2216401
Hutzler Bros	**Baltimore** 7271234
Jhaveri Bros	**Bombay** 327468

John Lewis	**London 6373434**
Jones & Guerno	**Agona 7726740**
Koninklijke Bijenkorf, NV	**Amsterdam 44848**
McKinlays	**Launceston 21811**
Macys	**New York 6954400**
Marks & Spencer	**London 9354422**
May Department Stores	**St Louis 4363300**
Milne & Choyce	**Auckland 74690**
Morum Bros	**Queenstown 2191**
Mothercare	**Watford 33577**
Myer	**Sydney 2389111**
Robinson & Co	**Singapore 92651**
Safeways	**Oakland 8913000**
Sainsburys	**London 9283355**
Saled Ismail Sayed Abdul Rasool	**Kuwait 433765**
Selfridges	**London 6291234**
W. H. Smith & Son	**London 3530277**
Société Française des Nouvelles Galeries Réunies	**Paris 8878250**
Steen & Strom	**Oslo 416800**
Tesco Stores	**Cheshunt 32222**
Trimmingham Bros	**Hamilton 11183**
Velasco Alonso	**Areciba 8780980**
Winns	**Sydney 310355**
Woolworths	**New York 2271000**
Woolworths	**Sydney 20653**

SING SOMETHING SIMPLE
30 of the world's top voices and their agents

For reasons best left undisclosed the world's most notorious
singer (in public that is), Florence Foster Jenkins, does not

feature in the list below. This Pennsylvania heiress, whose singing was variously described as 'the untrammeled swoop of some great bird' (*Saturday Review*), and 'in high notes, Mrs Jenkins sounds as if she was afflicted with low, nagging backache' (*Newseek*), once packed New York's Carnegie Hall with a concert which saw her in roles as varied as the Queen of the Night from the *Magic Flute* to a lusty Spanish damsel – and this when she had passed the age of seventy. She claimed that she owed her unique vocal range to a car accident. Few disagreed with her. For those at the other end of the singing ladder, try . . .

Bacquier, Gabriel	**Paris 2273384**
Bailey, Norman	**Bletchingley 48271**
Bailey, Pearl	**New York 5865100**
Baker, Dame Janet	**London 4864021**
Belafonte, Harry	**New York 7571660**
Berry, Walter	**Zurich 471988**
Blegen, Judith	**New York 4217676**
Borg, Kim	**Copenhagen 290731**
Borkh, Inge	**Heiden 912091**
Burrowes, Norma	**London 4857322**
Corelli, Franco	**London 4939158**
Davis, Sammy Jr	**Beverly Hills 5536895**
Del Monaco, Mario	**New York 7993100**
Dubai & Sharjah Singers	**Dubai 441019**
Edelmann, Otto	**Vienna 885563**
Evans, Sir Geraint	**Orpington 20529**
Frick, Gottlobb	**Oldbronn-Dürm 6508**
Gedda, Nicolai	**London 7345459**
Gobbi, Tito	**Rome 990996**
Greindl, Josef	**Munich 744506**
Harper, Heather	**London 2299166**
Home, Marilyn	**New York 7993100**
Kunz, Erich	**Vienna 322201**
Langdon, Michael	**Brighton 733120**

Milnes, Sherrill	**New York 2453530**
Norman, Jessye	**New York 5868135**
Pavarotti, Luciano	**Modena 351081**
Shirley-Quirk, John	**Flackwell Heath 21325**
Sinatra, Frank	**New York 8403500**
Sutherland, Dame Joan	**London 9375158**

S IS FOR SECURITY
10 world security services

A redoubtable regency detective, one G. Walsh, elevated the security services to new heights in the summer of 1797 when he resolutely followed William and Dorothy Wordsworth as they wandered about the Quantock Hills with their chum Coleridge, under the firm conviction that they were French spies. Laugh as we might, things haven't changed that much today, but for good measure these agencies can be of use.

Anti-Crime Security Service	**Perth 3891994**
Argus Security	**Dublin 781060**
Bureau of State Security (BOSS)	**Johannesburg 8364551**
CIA	**Washington DC 3511100**
Dominion Protection Services	**Auckland HSN37570**
FBI (Hawaii)	**Honolulu 5211411**
Inter-Globe Security	**London 9659741**
Maryland State Penitentiary	**Baltimore 8372135**
Mayne Nickless	**Sydney 920823**
Society for Former Special Agents of the FBI	**New York 6876222**

SKIN DEEP
or how to make the best of yourself wherever you are

Beauty may be skin deep and in the eye of the beholder, but it won't be all that long before the eye of the beholder will be getting a good look at you from the other end of the telephone line, and then your skin will need to be more thick than deep if you're not going to fly into a panic about your appearance. In certain establishments they specialize in these matters, of course. Get in early to save your peace of mind. At the same time don't overlook Henry Haskin's gentle advice, 'If a man hears much that a woman says, she is not beautiful.' You can't have it both ways.

Ballsbridge Beauty & Sauna Centre	**Dublin 683230**
Corla's Beauty Boutique	**Toronto 4834100**
Eddie Senz Mini Spa	**New York 7532326**
Genesis Beauty Centre	**Sydney 3891134**

London Lass Beauty Salon	**San Francisco 9221700**
Mimi's Too Beautiful Boutique	**Perth 3253309**
Nu-You Slimming & Beauty Salon	**Johannesburg 8692452**
Shrinkers Figure & Beauty Clinic	**Auckland 773655**
Yvonne's Beauty Centre	**Ras al-Khaimah 29540**

SKYSCRAPERS
10 of the world's tallest buildings

Chicago's Sears Roebuck tower is the world's tallest office building, while the world's largest office building is New York's World Trade Center with over 200 acres of office space.

Chrysler Building	**New York 6977400**
Eiffel Tower	**Paris 7054413**
Empire State Building	**New York 7363100**
First Canadian Place	**Toronto 8626100**
First National City Corp	**New York 5590467**
John Hancock Center	**Chicago 7513681**
Sears Roebuck Tower	**Chicago 8758300**
Sixty Wall Tower	**New York 3447538**
Waters Tower Plaza	**Chicago 4403460**
World Trade Center	**New York 4667377**

SKY WATCHERS
20 astronomers

According to Stephen Leacock, 'Astronomy teaches the correct use of the sun and planets.' For a different definition you might care to ring . . .

Babock, Horace	**Pasadena 5771122**
Bok, Bart	**Tucson 6262589**
Bourgeois, Paul	**Brussels 743058**
Delhaye, Jean	**Paris 3292112**
Denisse, Jean François	**Paris 6261630**
Goldberg, Leo	**Tucson 3275511**
Heckmann, Otto	**Hamburg 7221750**
Hewish, Anthony	**Comberton 2657**
Hulst, Hendrik	**Leiden 148333**
Jeffreys, Sir Harold	**Cambridge 3556153**
Kourganoff, Vladimir	**Paris 5405053**
Lovell, Sir Bernard	**Lower Withington 71321**
Massevitch, Alla	**Moscow 2315461**
Münch, Guido	**Heidelberg 5281**
Niniger, Harvey	**Sedona 2823613**
Oort, Jan	**Oegstgeest 154158**
Roberts, Water	**Boulder 4431230**
Rosseland, Suein	**Oslo 244760**
Sadler, Donald	**Cooden 3572**
Wilson, Robert	**Holmdel 9468518**

SOMETHING TO CHEW ON
6 makers of gum

American Chewing Gum	**Ardmore 5285900**
Gum Base	**New York 7685560**
Sweets Gum Base	**New York 7882645**

Topps Chewing Gum	**New York 7688900**
Wrigley de Mexico	**Naucalpan de Juarez 5765833**
W. M. Wrigley Jr	**Chicago 6442121**

SPACED OUT
a dozen astronauts

Eugene Cernan is one of the three men to have travelled faster than any other human being. He and his two colleagues aboard the Command Module of Apollo X touched 24,791 mph on their re-entry in May 1969. The rest of the list have travelled at some fairly spectacular speeds as well.

Aldrin, Edward (Buzz)	**Los Angeles 4764712**
Bean, Alan	**Houston 4832321**
Borman, Frank	**Miami 8732211**
Carr, Gerald	**Houston 5294921**
Cernan, Eugene	**Houston 4670741**
Collins, Michael	**Washington DC 3815766**
Conrad, Charles	**Englewood 7615705**
Garriot, Owen	**Houston 4830123**
Glenn, John	**Washington DC 2243353**
Irwin, James	**Colorado Springs 5741200**
Shepard, Alan	**Washington DC 7552320**
Worden, Alfred	**Washington DC 7552300**

Contact for former astronauts:

NASA	**Washington DC 7558364**

THE SPORT OF KINGS
10 of the world's race courses

Art Buchwald once described Ascot as 'so exclusive that it is the only race course in the world where the horses own the people'. To confirm this point of view and those about other famous courses, try ringing . . .

Ascot Race Course	**Ascot 22211**
Auckland Race Course	**Auckland 544069**
Cheltenham Race Course	**Cheltenham 23102**
Curragh Race Course	**Kildare 61559**
Downpatrick Race Course	**Downpatrick 2054**
Epsom Race Course	**Epsom 26311**
Goodwood Race Course	**Chichester 527107**
Harold Park (Trots)	**Sydney 6603688**
Karachi Race Course	**Karachi 515809**
Newmarket Race Course	**Newmarket 2762**

STAR TREK
40 leading actresses and their agents

'I got all the schooling any actress needs. That is, I learned to write enough to sign contracts.' Not everyone shares Hermione Gingold's opinion of herself or of her fellow stars, and here are forty who are likely to disagree for a start . . .

Ann-Margret	**Beverly Hills 2747451**
Bacall, Lauren	**New York 7573970**
Ball, Lucille	**Los Angeles 6502500**
Bancroft, Anne	**Los Angeles 5501234**
Bergen, Candice	**New York 7595202**
Black, Shirley (Temple)	**Washington DC 6320866**

Bloom, Claire	**London 2403086**
Christie, Julie	**London 6298080**
Cummings, Constance	**London 3520437**
Davis, Bette	**New York 7512107**
Day, Doris	**Beverly Hills 5501181**
Dench, Judi	**London 4914400**
Dunawaye, Fay	**Los Angeles 5504000**
Ekland, Britt	**London 9376575**
Farrow, Mia	**Los Angeles 2781572**
Fonda, Jane	**Beverly Hills 2747451**
Jackson, Glenda	**London 4371424**
Hampshire, Susan	**London 4394371**
Hawn, Goldie	**Beverly Hills 2747451**
Hepburn, Katherine	**New York 5865100**
Hunnicut, Gayle	**London 7349361**
Keaton, Diane	**Los Angeles 2746024**
Keith, Penelope	**London 4937570**
Ladd, Cheryl	**Beverly Hills 2747451**
Loren, Sophia	**Paris 2255332**
MacGraw, Ali	**Los Angeles 5504000**
MacLaine, Shirley	**New York 5565600**
Minnelli, Liza	**New York 7595202**
Moore, Mary Tyler	**Studio City 7638411**
Newton John, Olivia	**Los Angeles 5508232**
Plowright, Joan	**London 8367932**
Smith, Maggie	**London 7349361**
Streisand, Barbra	**Los Angeles 5504000**
Suzmann, Janet	**London 7349361**
Swanson, Gloria	**New York PL70720**
Taylor, Elizabeth	**New York 4216720**
Tcherina, Ludmila	**Paris 3591833**
Tutin, Dorothy	**London 7373444**
Ullmann, Liv	**Los Angeles 5501060**
York, Susannah	**London 6298080**

STRUNG UP
5 leading guitarists and their agents

The world's largest guitar is just over ten feet tall, though the musicians listed here usually make do with somewhat smaller instruments.

Bream, Julian	**London 9352331**
Harrison, George	**London 2359981**
McCartney, Paul	**London 4396621**
Segovia	**London 4864021**
Williams, John	**London 9352331**

SUFFER THE LITTLE CHILDREN
8 ways to save your marriage and your sanity

Babysitters Unlimited	**London 7307777/8**
Childcare Switchboard	**San Francisco 2827858**
Childminders	**Dublin 767981**
Dial-an-angel	**Sydney 4671511**
Dynamic Personnel	**Toronto 7872276**
Good Companions	**Johannesburg 7885680**
Jack & Jill	**Perth 3845955**
Part-Time Child Care	**New York 8794343**

TEE-UP
5 of the world's champion golfers

Jack Nicklaus holds the record (with Raymond Floyd) for the lowest score in the US Master's, while at the other end of the scale one A. J. Lewis triumphed at Peacehaven in Sussex in 1890 when he took 156 putts on one green alone during a competition!

Miller, Johnny
Nicklaus, Jack

Napa 2552970
North Palm Beach
6263900

Palmer, Arnold	**Latrobe 5377751**
Player, Gary	**London 4930816**
Trevino, Lee	**El Paso 5893466**

TEMPERANCE LINE
13 makers of non-alcoholic drinks to keep you on the wagon when you're most tempted to jump off

'Work is the curse of the drinking classes,' said Oscar Wilde, and who, faced with a difficult meeting in the afternoon or the prospect of another half-day's grind, would disagree with him? Only the makers of soft drinks, you might argue, and who better to ring in moments when your resolve shows signs of weakening?

Associated Products & Distribution	**Sydney 20578**
Bermuda Mineral Water Co	**Hamilton 16151**
Canada Dry	**Downsview 6339440**
Coca-Cola, Puerto Rico	**Hato Rey 7671433**
Coca-Cola Export Corp	**Rizal 998701**
Crush International	**Toronto 7513333**
Dad's Root Beer Co	**Chicago 4634600**
Dr Pepper Co	**Dallas 8240331**
Pepsi Cola	**Purchase 2532000**
Pure Spring (Canada)	**Ottawa 2369961**
Schweppes (USA)	**Stamford 3290911**
Seven-up Export Corp	**New York 4259077**
Yoo-Hoo Chocolate Beverage Corp	**Carlstadt 9330070**

TOP DOG
a dozen prime ministers

The Rt Hon William Pulteney, Earl of Bath, held the office of Prime Minister for a record three days, at the end of which no one wanted to join him, so he packed it in. Doubtless the incumbents listed below would have been willing to give him a few tips, and who knows, they may do the same for interested callers.

Prime Minister of:

Australia	**Canberra 730416**
Belgium	**Brussels 5138020**
Czechoslovakia	**Prague 5138020**
Denmark	**Copenhagen 113038**
France	**Paris 5668000**
Germany, West	**Bonn 1051**
Ireland	**Dublin 767571**
Italy	**Rome 6779**
Japan	**Tokyo 5810101**
Swaziland	**Mbabane 2251**
Turkey	**Ankara 283120**
UK	**London 9301234**

TRIGGER HAPPY
firearms and ammo for your personal arsenal

Billy the Kid's Colt, James Bond's Beretta and the sub-machine guns of the SAS, not to mention the hundreds of other small arms available on the general and illicit market, all started life in the world's great armaments factories. Some names are almost legendary, others prefer a discreet seclusion. But if you're planning a coup d'état, or just fancy a little rougher-than-usual shooting, these are some of the numbers you may need.

Bangor Punta Operations	**Greenwich 6613900**
Beretta, Gardone	**Gardone 837261**
Brandt Armaments	**Paris 3591887**
Colt Firearms	**Hartford 2788550**
Firearms Co	**Bridgwater 8211**
Giat	**Saint-Cloud 6025200**
Harrington & Richardson	**Worcester 7916241**
International Armament	**Alexandria 5484437**
RAMO	**Nashville 2448690**
Simmel	**Castelfranco 45741**
SNIA	**Rome 4680**
Sterling	**Dagenham 5952226**
Sturm, Ruger & Co	**Southport 2597843**

TUNING IN
a dozen orchestras

At one concert given in the summer of 1872 Johann Strauss the younger conducted an orchestra of 987 instruments, including 400 first violins. The orchestras given below will offer more limited services, but they'll also be easier to accommodate.

Aarhus By-Orkester	**Aarhus 127122**
London Philharmonic	**London 4869771**
London Symphony Orchestra	**London 4398427**
New Philharmonic Orchestra	**London 5809961**
New York Philharmonic	**New York 5808700**

Orchestra de Paris	**Paris 7582732**
Orchestre National de Belgique	**Brussels 7339455**
Orchestre National de France	**Paris 2242603**
Philadelphia Orchestra	**Philadelphia 8931900**
Royal Philharmonic Orchestra	**London 6294078**
Silvester Orchestra	**London 7228191**
Soenderjyllands Symfoniorkester	**Soenderberg 426161**

UP, UP, AND AWAY
around the world with 50 airports

The importance of knowing about the airports from which
and to which you fly is vividly illustrated by the story of one
Italian resident of San Francisco who took a flight home to see
his family after many years' absence. The flight plan,
unbeknown to him, included a re-fuelling stop in New York.
Mistaking this for his destination, the man left his plane and
began searching New York for his relatives in the firm belief
that he was in Rome. The absence of that city's historic
landmarks, not to mention the proliferation of 'Italians' with
a fluent command of English, did nothing to shake his resolve.
Now, had he known a little more about Kennedy Airport in
the first place, he could have saved himself hours of confusion
and a return flight to San Francisco.

Adelaide Airport	**Adelaide 438071**
Akyab Airport	**Akyab 170**
Assab Airport	**Assab 2**
Auckland International	**Auckland 666166**
Baghdad International	**Baghdad 518888**
Bamako Airport	**Bamako 22701**
Bangkok International	**Bangkok 796200**
Banjul/Yundum Airport	**Yundum 745**
Berlin, Tempelhof	**Berlin 6909307**
Brisbane Airport	**Brisbane 685333**
Brunei International	**Brunei 3141**
Cairo Airport	**Cairo 64384**
Calcutta Airport	**Calcutta 573187**
Canberra Airport	**Canberra 731603**

Casablanca/Nouasser Airport	**Casablanca 39040**
Chittagong Airport	**Chittagong 85991**
Doha Airport	**Doha 4881**
Entebbe Airport	**Entebbe 2516**
Freeport International	**Bahamas 3527921**
Frimaker Airport	**Liechtenstein 23348**
Gatwick Airport	**London 6884211**
Granada Airport	**Granada 273400**
Heathrow Airport	**London 7594321**
Ho Chi Minh City Airport	**Ho Chi Minh City 43179**
Hong Kong International	**Kowloon 820211**
Juba Airport	**Juba 6944**
Jujuy Airport	**Jujuy 91101**
Kabul Airport	**Kabul 25541**
J. F. Kennedy Airport	**New York 6564520**
Kerkyra Airport	**Corfu 22952**
Lahore Airport	**Lahore 71090**
Luanda Airport	**Luanda 24141**
Lusaka International	**Lusaka 74331**
Managua/Las Mercedes Airport	**Managua 91281**
Maputu Airport	**Maputu 732153**
O'Hare International	**Chicago 6862200**
Okecie Airport	**Warsaw 461182**
Ougadougou Airport	**Ougadougou 216415**
Phnom-Penh Airport	**Phnom-Penh 23703**
Port Stanley Aerodrome	**Port Stanley 219**
Riyadh International	**Riyadh 580**
Singapore Airport	**Singapore 82321**
Sofia Airport	**Sofia 451121**
Tahiti-Faa Airport	**French Polynesia 28081**
Tirana Airport	**Tirana 2792**
Vagar Airport	**Thørshavn 92**

Venice Airport	**Venice 957333**
Yaoundé Airport	**Yaoundé 222500**
Yeşilköy Airport	**Istanbul 737388**
Zarzaitine/In Amenas	
Airport	**In Amenas 4**

VOICES OF THE PEOPLE
30 of the world's politicians and statesmen

According to Bill Vaughan 'A statesman is any politician it's considered safe to name a school after', though Bob Edwards put a different gloss on the explanation when he said, 'Now I know what a statesman is; he's a dead politician. We need more statesmen.' No matter which side of the fence you may stand on, assuming that you're not sitting astride it, politicians are here to stay and since it's unlikely that we'll be able to beat them, here are the numbers of some you may care to join.

Agnew, Spiro	**Arnold 7571152**
Benn, Anthony Wedgwood	**London 2193000**
Boersma, Jacob	**The Hague 469470**
Brown, Edmund	**Sacramento 4454711**
Callaghan, James	**London 2193000**
Chan, Julius	**Port Moresby 211622**
Chipp, Hon Don	**Canberra 622521**
Cosgrave, Liam	**Dublin 761573**
Goldwater, Barry	**Scottsdale 2614086**
Hailsham of St Marylebone, Baron	**London 7882256**
Kennedy, Edward	**Washington DC 2244543**
Kissinger, Dr Henry	**Washington DC 8720300**
Luns, Joseph	**Brussels 410040**
McGovern, George	**Mitchell 9967563**
Nixon, Richard	**San Clemente 4920011**
Raisani, Sardar	**Quetta 70661**
Ram, Hon Jagjivan	**New Delhi 376555**
Renshaw, Jock	**Sydney 2302111**

Rockefeller, John D.	**Charleston 3483456**
Rockefeller, Nelson	**New York 2473700**
Roem, Mohammad	**Jakarta-Pusat 343393**
Rusk, Dean	**Athens 5496471**
Speaker of the House (US Senate)	**Washington DC 2253505**
Stephens, Robert	**Piggs Peak 9**
Todd, Garfield	**Shabami 01222**
Tugenhadt, Christopher	**Brussels 6497867**
Wallace, George	**Montgomery 3823511**
Winneke, Sir Henry	**Melbourne 639971**
Withers, Rt Hon Reg	**Perth 3258449**
Žarković, Vidoje	**Belgrade 331279**

WARFARE HARDWARE
15 manufacturers of the world's weapons systems

The Chinese defended the city of K'ai-Fung-Fu from Mongol attack in 1232 by firing rockets at the attackers. The Mongols for their own part had already developed primitive hand-grenades by this time. Missiles have come a long way since the thirteenth century. To find out just how far, contact . . .

AEG Telefunken	**Frankfurt 6690**
Aerosystem Electronic	**Zurich 814117**
Alvaradio Industries	**Los Angeles 4783555**
Baur and Stroud	**Glasgow 9549601**
Bofors Ordnance	**Bofors 36000**
EDO International	
Division	**New York 4456000**
Elbit Computers	**Haifa 514211**
Euromissile	**Châtillon 6571244**
Ferranti Computer System	**Bracknell 3232**
Hollandse	
Signaalapparaten	**Hengelo 88111**
Litton Systems	**Toronto 2491231**
Marconi Space &	
Defence Systems	**London 9542311**
Officine Galileo	**Florence 47961**
Plessey Co	**Ilford 4783040**
Racal Electronics	**Bracknell 3244**

WATCH IT
10 leading manufacturers of wrist-watches

If you believe that small is beautiful, there's only one watch for you: the fifteen-jewel Jaeger Le Coultre which measures half by three sixteenths of an inch. If your demands are something other than those of size, try . . .

Aichi Clock & Electric Implement Mfg Co	**Nagoya 6615151**
Audemars Piquet & Cie	**Le Brassus 855033**
Benrus Corp	**Ridgefield 4380333**
Bulova Watch Co	**New York 5810400**
Citizen Watch Co	**Tokyo 3421231**
Eterna Ltd	**Grenchen 82171**
Longines	**St Imier 412422**
Rhythm Watch Co	**Tokyo 8337311**
Rolex	**Bienne 22611**
Timex	**Greenwich 6613227**

WHAT A BORE
5 manufacturers of boring machinery

Fulmer Co	**Fort Thomas 4411174**
Giddings & Lewis Machine Tool Co	**Fond du Lac 9219400**
Kearney & Trekker	**Milwaukee 4768300**
Litton Industries, New Britain Machine Tool Div	**New Britain 2291641**
Standard-Modern Tool	**Toronto 7872494**

WHISKY GALORE
25 makers of fine spirits from advocaat to whisky

When it comes to drink things certainly aren't what they once were. In the heady days of the early eighteenth century the consumption of gin in England alone shot up from 2 million to 5 million gallons in just twenty years – and gin was the drink of the working classes. The better-off knocked back brandy or port to the tune of five or six bottles a man. Dr Johnson is credited with sinking thirty-six glasses of port in one session without even budging from his seat, an astonishing feat of both consumption and containment. Today our tastes are more catholic, and this list offers a range of exotic tipples and some old favourites to keep at hand in moments of need.

Angove's	Renmark 51311
Bacardi	Nassau 7841560
Ballantines	Dumbarton 3111
John Begg	Glasgow 2214518
Benmore Distilleries	Glasgow 2213254
Bols	Amsterdam 8141
Burnett	London 4932061

Captain Morgan Rum	**Montreal 8495271**
Crawford	**Edinburgh 5543161**
Cusenier	**Paris 3713684**
Distilleries Co	**Edinburgh 2292468**
Distillerie Stock	**Trieste 414181**
Esbeco	**Stamford 3482656**
Fraser MacDonald	**Glasgow 3325341**
Glenmore Distilleries	**Louisville 5899121**
Guyana Distilleries	**Georgetown 66171**
Haig	**Markinch 404**
Heering	**Copenhagen SU8585**
Jamaica Rums	**Kingston 9323440**
Kinloch Distillery	**Glasgow 3326525**
Metaxa	**Athens 8016712**
Mohan Meakens	**Lucknow 22422**
Seagrams	**Montreal 8495271**
Société Martell	**Cognac 824444**
United Distilleries	**Sydney 3872838**

WORLD AID
15 relief and other helping agencies

International help comes in many shapes and sizes – from the famine-relief kitchen in India which served 1,200,000 meals a day in April 1973, to the village well that can be bored for only a few hundred pounds. These are some of the groups and organizations responsible for keeping the needs of the deprived before our eyes.

Amnesty International	**London 8367788**
Anti-Apartheid Movement	**London 5805311**
Anti-Slavery Society for the Protection of Human Rights	**London 9356498**

Assembly of Captive European Nations	**New York 7513850**
Care	**New York 6863110**
International League for Human Rights	**New York 9729554**
League of Red Cross Societies	**Geneva 345580**
Oxfam	**Oxford 5677**
Salvation Army, International Head-quarters of the	**London 2365222**
United Nations Disaster Relief Coordinator	**Geneva 310211**
United Nations High Commissioner for Refugees	**Geneva 346011**
World Council of Churches	**Geneva 333400**
World Food Council	**Rome 5795**
World Health Organ-ization	**Geneva 346061**
World Peace Council	**Helsinki 649004**

WORLD CUP
24 national football bodies

Not every country plays the game in quite the same way and in order to follow international events it's as well to know how your opponents operate. For instance two rival sides, both seeking promotion in the Yugoslav league, won their respective final games by generous margins. One team scored 134 goals to 1, the others notched up a more modest 88-0. Both had taken the precaution of getting their opponents and the referees to agree to the arrangement before kick-off.

Czechoslovak Football	**Prague 249841**
Dansk Boldspil	**Copenhagen 424540**
Deutscher Fussball-Bund	**Frankfurt 631063**
Federação Portuguesa de Futebol	**Lisbon 328207**
Federation Albanique de Football	**Tirana 7256**
Federation Bulgare de Football	**Sofia 8651**
Federation de Football de l'URSS	**Moscow 2915796**
Fédération Française de Football	**Paris 7206540**

Federation Hellenique de Football	**Athens 3622220**
Federation Hongroise de Football	**Budapest 225817**
Federation Turque de Football	**Ankara 24393415**
Federazione Italiana Giuoco Calcio	**Rome 8491**
Football Association of Iceland	**Reykjavik 84444**
Football Association of Ireland	**Dublin 766864**
Liechtensteiner Fussball- verband	**Vaduz 23879**
Malta Football Association	**Valletta 22697**
Norges Fotballforbund	**Oslo 469830**
Oesterreicher Fussball- Bund	**Vienna 571536**
Polish Football Association	**Warsaw 289344**
Real Federación Española de Futbol	**Madrid 2391000**
Schweizerischer Fussball- verband	**Berne 446223**
Suomen Palloliito	**Helsinki 441281**
Svenska Fotballförbendet	**Stockholm 272500**
Union Royale des Sociétés de Football Association	**Brussels 2300730**

WRITERS' GUILD
20 writers and journalists

'If I had to give young writers advice, I'd say don't listen to writers talking about writing,' once commented Lillian

Hellman, and, if she's right, you'll have to come up with some other excuse for telephoning . . .

Abe, Kobo	**Tokyo 033003833**
Abzug, Bella	**New York 4221414**
Bellow, Saul	**Chicago 7533852**
Beonish, Peter	**Berlin 2591**
Bernstein, Carl	**New York 2494417**
Boldizsar, Ivan	**Budapest 136857**
Bomefoy, Yves	**Paris 6068812**
Brandreth, Gyles	**London 7274290**
Bulatovic, Vukoje	**Belgrade 329367**
Cameron, James	**London 5865340**
Conchon, Georges	**Paris 228996**
Day, Sir Robin	**London 7438000**
Dedijer, Vladimir	**Ljubljana 261729**
Fraser, Lady Antonia	**London 2621011**
Friendly, Fred	**Riverdale 5734848**
Gammal, Ali	**Cairo 48887**
Gordey, Michel	**Paris 0337982**
Kemal, Yashar	**Istanbul 790887**
Osmańcyk, Edmund	**Warsaw 315797**
Poleroi, Boris	**Moscow 2558922**

YES, MINISTER
25 government departments from Outer Space to Family Planning

With unemployment rising at home your thoughts might sensibly turn to less troubled parts of the world, Kuwait for instance. On the other hand the Ministry of Labour in Iran may not be your immediate choice. For first-hand, up-to-the-minute information, or just a chat, dial . . .

Agriculture and Food Ministry	**Budapest 113000**
Attorney General	**Washington DC 6654000**
Bureau of Indian Affairs	**Washington DC 7378200**
Diwan of Royal Protocol	**Muscat 722621**
Fisheries Dept, Government of Maharastra	**Bombay 312061**
Foreigners' Registration Office	**Benares 64333**
John F. Kennedy Space Center	**Florida 8673333**
Kuwait Projects	**Safat 44289**
Lyndon B. Johnson Space Center	**Houston 4834588**
Minister for Business and Consumer Affairs	**Canberra 730414**
Minister for National Resources	**Canberra 730413**
Minister for Overseas Trade	**Canberra 614111**
Ministerio de Marina	**Madrid 2343233**
Ministry of Aviation	**Madrid 2432420**

Ministry of Commerce, Industry and Shipping	Copenhagen 121197
Ministry of Communications	Baghdad 7766041
Ministry of Culture and Science	Athens 8081018
Ministry of Education	Zomba 611
Ministry of Family and Consumption	Oslo 119090
Ministry of Labour and Social Affairs	Tehran 970051
Ministry of Transport	Bonn 721
Ministry of Transport and Power	Dublin 789522
National Aeronautics and Space Agency (NASA)	Washington DC 7553000
Pakistan National Council for the Arts	Islamabad 22368
Transport and Post Ministry	Budapest 220220

YOU GOT RHYTHM
15 of the world's conductors and their agents

'Why do we in England engage at our concerts so many third-rate continental conductors when we have so many second-rate ones of our own?' So said Sir Thomas Beecham, no doubt embracing in that damning observation not a few of those listed below.

Atzman, Moshe	London 6246322
Boskovsky, Willi	Vienna 726459
Boulez, Pierre	New York 5808700

Erdélyi, Miklós	**Budapest 655160**
Frémaux, Louis	**Paris 2247587**
Guest, Douglas	**Minchinhampton 883191**
Haitink, Bernard	**London 4398427**
Kostelanetz, André	**New York 7873700**
Levine, James	**New York 3976900**
Lutoslawski, Witold	**Warsaw 392390**
Mackerras, Sir Charles	**London 2864047**
Ormandy, Eugene	**Philadelphia 8931900**
Ozawa, Seiji	**Boston 2661492**
Previn, André	**London 4398427**
Strauss, Paul	**New York 9438722**

YOUR LIFE IN THEIR HANDS
15 hospitals from Paris to Peking

Don't be fobbed off by those who tell you that there's nothing to going into hospital; there's everything, especially if it's not one on home soil. As Jean Kerr wrote in *Operation, Operation*: 'One of the most difficult things to contend with in a hospital is the assumption on the part of the staff that because you have lost your gall bladder you have also lost your mind' – exactly. If you can't speak the lingo either, your problems are almost insurmountable. There's all the more reason, therefore, for doing a little checking up in advance.

Acupuncture Service Center	**Los Angeles 2225090**
American Hospital	**Istanbul 467005**
American Hospital	**Paris MIA6800**
Anti-Imperialist Hospital	**Peking 553731**
British-American Hospital	**Lima 23000**
French Hospital	**Izmir 33934**
International Hospital	**Kobe 335697**
Jam Hospital	**Tehran 833080**
Ochsner Clinic	**New Orleans 8347070**
Outram General Hospital	**Singapore 73141**
Shanaz Hospital	**Mashad 30001**
Taipei Chung Hsing Hospital	**Taipei 545641**
Tokyo Medical & Surgical Centre	**Tokyo 4314121**
Tokyo Sanatorium Hospital	**Tokyo 3926151**
Yodogama Christian Hospital	**Osaka 3222250**

ZOO CALL

15 world zoos, wildlife parks, and other animal centres

Telephones haven't made much of an impression on the world of nature, which is no doubt a good thing. There's one wildlife park in Namibia which covers an area of almost 38,500 square miles, where phones are very thin on the ground. And if you fancy having a chat with a tiger in northern India, your best bet would be to ring District Naintal 76 and hope for the best.

African Lion Safari	**Sydney 741113**
American Kennel Club	**New York 4819200**
Animal Talent Scouts	**New York 2432700**
Animal Welfare Board of India	**Madras 74307**
Auckland Zoological Park	**Auckland 764785**
Chicago Zoo	**Chicago 2944660**
Eton College, Beagles Kennels	**Slough 24968**
Field Director, Project Tiger	**District Naintal 76**
Kaziranga Wildlife Sanctuary	**Kaziranga 3**
London Zoo	**London 7223333**
Long Island Game Farm Zoological Park	**Long Island 7277443**
Taronga Zoo	**Sydney 9692295**
Wildlife Warden	**Ram Nagar District 76**
World Wildlife Fund	**Washington DC 4819200**
Zoological Garden	**Karachi 70908**

DIALLING THE WORLD

The gazetteer that follows should help you identify the country you want if you're a bit hazy about where on the globe to find Yundum or Dušanbe, or any of the other places listed in the book

Once you've found your country you're ready to go. Start by checking whether it can be dialled direct. (For British readers, a nation-by-nation guide to STD codes for every country in the world follows on page 181. Other readers

should check their telephone code book.) If it can't, the international operator will make the connection for you. If *you can dial direct* this is the sequence to follow.

Dial: International prefix
Country Code
Area Code
The number you want
to call

If your code book is of no help, the international operator will give you those codes not listed. Don't be impatient if you have to wait for up to one minute before your number starts to ring. Use the time wisely. It's the last chance you'll have to think of what you're going to say when the receiver's lifted at the other end!

A

Aargau Switzerland
Aarhus Denmark
Abu Dhabi Abu Dhabi
Accra Ghana
Addis Ababa Ethiopia
Adelaide Australia
Agona Guam
Agra India
Ahmadi Kuwait
Aichi Japan
Aix-les-Bains France
Ajman Ajman
Akron USA
Akureyri Iceland
Akyab Burma
Albuquerque USA
Aldeburgh UK
Alès France
Alexandria Egypt
Alexandria USA
Allahabad India
Amman Jordan

Amritsar India
Amsterdam Netherlands
Ancy le France France
Ankara Turkey
Ardmore USA
Areciba Puerto Rico
Arlington USA
Armonk USA
Arnold USA
Arundel UK
Ascot UK
Ashcroft Canada
Ashland USA
Athens Greece
Atlanta USA
Auchterarder UK
Auckland New Zealand
Austin USA

B

Bad Kreuznach West
Germany

Baghdad Iraq
Bahrain Bahrain
Baltimore USA
Bamako Mali
Bamburgh UK
Bandar Seri Begawan
  Brunei
Banff USA
Bangkok Thailand
Barcelona Spain
Barnard Castle UK
Basle Switzerland
Baslow UK
Battle Creek USA
Bayreuth West Germany
Beirut Lebanon
Belfast UK
Belfort France
Belgrade Yugoslavia
Belleville USA
Benares India
Benton Harbor USA
Berchtesgaden West
  Germany
Bergheim/Erft West
  Germany
Berkhamsted UK
Berkley USA
Berlin West Germany
Bethesda USA
Bethlehem USA
Beverly Hills USA
Bidford-on-Avon UK
Bienne Switzerland
Billancourt France
Birmingham UK

Blair Atholl UK
Bletchingley UK
Bofors Sweden
Bogota Colombia
Bologna Italy
Bombay India
Bon Juan Puerto Rico
Bonn West Germany
Bordeaux France
Boston USA
Boulder USA
Bracknell UK
Braemar UK
Braintree USA
Bratislava Czechoslovakia
Breda Netherlands
Bremen West Germany
Brescia Italy
Bridgwater UK
Brighton UK
Brisbane Australia
Bristol USA
Bruges Belgium
Brunei Brunei
Brussels Belgium
Bucharest Romania
Budapest Hungary
Buenos Aires Argentina
Buffalo USA
Bulawayo Zimbabwe
Burbank USA
Burggaben West
  Germany

C
Cairo Egypt

Calcutta India
Caldbeck UK
Calver City USA
Cambridge UK
Cambridge USA
Camden USA
Canberra Australia
Cannes France
Cape Town South Africa
Caracas Venezuela
Carlstadt USA
Carnoustie UK
Casablanca Morocco
Castelfranco Italy
Causeway Zimbabwe
Cawdor UK
Chantilly France
Charleston USA
Charlottesville USA
Chaska USA
Châtillon France
Cheltenham UK
Cheshunt UK
Chevington UK
Chichester UK
Chittagong Bangladesh
Cholderton UK
Claremont USA
Clermont-Ferrand
  France
Cleveland USA
Clifford UK
Cochin India
Cognac France
Cologne West Germany
Colombia USA

Colombo Sri Lanka
Colorado Springs USA
Comberton UK
Concord USA
Condom France
Cooden UK
Copenhagen Denmark
Corfu Greece
Cork Ireland
Courcouronnes France
Cranleigh UK
Croydon UK

D

Dagenham UK
Dallas USA
Damascus Syria
Dammam Saudi Arabia
Dar-es-Salaam Tanzania
Darjeeling India
Darmstadt West
  Germany
Dearborn USA
Dearfield USA
Deauville France
Delphi Greece
Denver USA
Detroit USA
Dinant Belgium
District Naintal India
Dodge City USA
Doha Qatar
Dortmund West
  Germany
Downpatrick Ireland
Downsview Canada

Drammer Norway
Dresden East Germany
Dubai Dubai
Dublin Ireland
Duluth USA
Dumbarton UK
Durban South Africa
Dursley UK
Dušanbe USSR
Düsseldorf West
  Germany

E
East Hanover USA
Edinburgh UK
Eferding Austria
Eindhoven Netherlands
El Dorado USA
El Paso USA
Englewood USA
Entebbe Uganda
Epernay France
Epsom UK
Essen West Germany

F
Fairfield USA
Flackwell Heath UK
Flagstaff USA
Florence Italy
Fond du Lac USA
Fontainebleau France
Fort Thomas USA
Fort Wayne USA
Foxrock Ireland
Frankfurt West Germany

Frindlay USA
Frome UK
Fujairah Fujairah
Fürth/Bay West Germany

G
Gardone Italy
Garroc Australia
Geneva Switzerland
Georgetown Guyana
Gilberton Australia
Girdwood USA
Glasgow UK
Glen Falls USA
Glenrothes UK
Glenview USA
Gothenburg Sweden
Göttingham-Geismar
  West Germany
Grafton Australia
Grahamstown South
  Africa
Grahamstown
  Zimbabwe
Granada Spain
Grand Rapids USA
Graz Austria
Great Missenden UK
Green Bay USA
Greenville USA
Greewich USA
Grenchen Switzerland
Gstaad Switzerland
Guatemala City
  Guatemala
Guayaquil Ecuador

Gwalior India
Gyttorp Sweden

Houston USA
Hunt Valley USA

H

Hadleigh UK
Hague, The Netherlands
Haifa Israel
Halifax Canada
Hamburg West Germany
Hamden USA
Hamilton Bermuda
Hamilton Canada
Hanoi Vietnam
Hanover USA
Harare Zimbabwe
Hartford USA
Hato Rey Puerto Rico
Havana Cuba
Havant UK
Hayward USA
Headingham UK
Heidelberg West
  Germany
Hellerup Denmark
Helsingor Denmark
Helsinki Finland
Hengelo Netherlands
Heraklion Greece
Hershey USA
Hinsdale USA
Hiroshima Japan
Ho Chi Minh City
  Vietnam
Holmdel USA
Hong Kong Hong Kong
Honolulu USA

I

Ilford UK
In Amenas Algeria
Independence USA
Inverary UK
Istanbul Turkey
Islamabad Pakistan
Isleworth UK
Ithaca USA
Iver UK
Iver Heath UK
Izmir Turkey

J

Jackson USA
Jaffna Sri Lanka
Jaipur India
Jakarta Indonesia
Jakarta-Pusat Indonesia
Jamaica Plains USA
Jayanagar India
Jeddah Saudi Arabia
Jersey (Channel Islands)
  UK
Jerusalem Israel
Johannesburg South
  Africa
Johore Malaysia
Juba Sudan

K

Kabul Afghanistan
Kalamazoo USA

Kampala Uganda
Kansas City USA
Kaohsiung Taiwan
Karachi Pakistan
Karlsruhe West Germany
Kathmandu Nepal
Kaziranga India
Kellogg USA
Kelso UK
Kenmore Australia
Khartoum Sudan
Kilchberg Switzerland
Kildare Ireland
Kingston Jamaica
Kingston-upon-Thames
  UK
Kintbury UK
Kitzbuhl Austria
Knipton UK
Kobe Japan
Kowloon Hong Kong
Kuala Lumpur Malaysia
Kumasi Ghana
Kuwait Kuwait
Kwaluseni Swaziland
Kyoto Japan

L
Lagos Nigeria
Lagos Portugal
Lahore Pakistan
Las Palmas Spain
Las Vegas USA
Latrobe USA
Launceston Australia
Laurian Greece

Lausanne Switzerland
Le Brassus Switzerland
Leiden Netherlands
Leningrad USSR
Lenzburg Switzerland
Lewes UK
Le Zoute Belgium
Liechtenstein
  Liechtenstein
Liège Belgium
Lima Peru
Limerick Ireland
Limpsfield UK
Lincoln USA
Linköping Sweden
Linz Austria
Lisbon Portugal
Livorno Italy
Ljubljana Yugoslavia
Lodsworth UK
London UK
Long Crendon UK
Long Island USA
Los Angeles USA
Louisville USA
Louvrain Belgium
Lower Withington UK
Lowestoft UK
Luanda Angola
Lucerne Switzerland
Lucknow India
Lusaka Zambia
Luxembourg
  Luxembourg
Lymington UK

M

Madras India
Madrid Spain
Maidenhead UK
Maidstone UK
Malvern UK
Mammoth Lakes USA
Managua Nicaragua
Manchester UK
Mandalay Burma
Manila Philippines
Maputu Mozambique
Markinch UK
Marrheeze Netherlands
Marseilles France
Mashad Iran
Mayaguez Puerto Rico
Mbabane Swaziland
Melbourne Australia
Memphis USA
Menlo Park USA
Menton France
Meteora Greece
Mexico City Mexico
Miami USA
Middletown USA
Milan Italy
Milwaukee USA
Minchinhampton UK
Minneapolis USA
Mitchell USA
Modena Italy
Mohenjodaro Pakistan
Monrovia Liberia
Mons Belgium
Monte Carlo Monaco

Montgomery USA
Montreal Canada
Montreux Switzerland
Morstel-Antwerp
  Belgium
Moscow USSR
Mount Coot-tha Australia
Much Hadham UK
Munich West Germany
Muscat Oman
Myoma Burma

N

Nagoya Japan
Nairobi Kenya
Nancy France
Napa USA
Naples Italy
Nashville USA
Nassau Bahamas
Naucalpan de Juarez
  Mexico
N'Djamena Chad
Ndola Zambia
Neuilly-sur-Seine France
Neuschwanstein bei
  Füsen West Germany
Newark USA
New Britain USA
New Delhi India
New Haven USA
Newmarket UK
New Orleans USA
Newport UK
Newtownards Ireland
New York USA

Niagara Falls Canada
Nice France
Nicosia Cyprus
Noorwijk Netherlands
Norfolk USA
North Palm Beach USA
Nottingham UK

O

Oak Brook USA
Oakland USA
Oestgeest Netherlands
Oldbronn-Dürm West
 Germany
Olympia Greece
Omaha USA
Oporto Portugal
Orchard Park USA
Orpington UK
Osaka Japan
Oslava Vrata
 Czechoslovakia
Oslo Norway
Ottawa Canada
Ouagadougou Upper
 Volta
Oxford UK

P

Pacific Palisades USA
Palatine USA
Palma Spain
Palmerston North New
 Zealand
Panama City Panama
Par UK

Paris France
Pasadena USA
Peking China
Penang Malaysia
Penzance UK
Perlis Malaysia
Persepolis Iran
Perth Australia
Perugia Italy
Philadelphia USA
Phnom-Penh
 Kampuchea
Piggs Peak Swaziland
Pittsburgh USA
Pontiac USA
Porthcawl UK
Port Moresby Papua
 New Guinea
Port-of-Spain Trinidad
 and Tobago
Portsmouth UK
Port Stanley Falkland
 Islands
Poughkeepsie USA
Prague Czechoslovakia
Pretoria South Africa
Princeton USA
Providence USA
Provo USA
Purchase USA

Q

Queenstown South
 Africa
Quetta Pakistan
Quito Ecuador

R

Radlett UK
Radnor USA
Ram Nagar District India
Randberg South Africa
Ras al-Khaimah Ras al-Khaimah
Rawalpindi Pakistan
Reims France
Renmark Australia
Reykjavik Iceland
Richmond Australia
Richmond UK
Ridgefield USA
Rio de Janeiro Brazil
Rio Grande Brazil
Riverdale USA
Riyadh Saudi Arabia
Rizal Philippines
Roanne France
Rochester USA
Rogers USA
Rome Italy
Rotherham UK
Rotterdam Netherlands
Rottweil-Allstadt West Germany
Royan France
Rungsted Kyst Denmark
Ruwi Oman

S

Saarbrucken West Germany
Sacramento USA
St Andrews UK
St Anne's-on-Sea UK
Saint-Claud France
Saint Emilion France
Saint Imier Switzerland
St Louis USA
St Peters Australia
Salzburg Austria
San Clemente USA
San Diego USA
San Francisco USA
San José Costa Rica
San Juan Puerto Rico
San Mateo USA
San Salvador El Salvador
San Sebastian Spain
São Paolo Brazil
Sarajevo Yugoslavia
Scone UK
Scottsdale USA
Seattle USA
Sedona USA
Seoul South Korea
Seraing Belgium
Shabami Zimbabwe
Sharjah Sharjah
Sherman USA
Shiraz Iran
Shizuoka Japan
Singapore Singapore
Slough UK
Soeburg Denmark
Soenderberg Denmark
Sofia Bulgaria
Southfield USA
Southport USA

Soweto South Africa
Sparta Greece
Springfield USA
Staindrop UK
Stamford USA
Stavanger Norway
Stellenbosch South Africa
Stockholm Sweden
Stony Brook USA
Strachur UK
Strasbourg France
Stratford-upon-Avon
   UK
Studio City USA
Stuttgart West Germany
Sunderland UK
Sutton Canada
Sydney Australia

T
Taipei Taiwan
Tampa USA
Tarzana USA
Taunton UK
Tegucigalpa Honduras
Tehran Iran
Tel Aviv Israel
Thessaloniki Greece
Thompsonville USA
Thørshavn Faeroe Islands
Tibaron USA
Tikkakoski Finland
Tirana Albania
Tokyo Japan
Toronto Canada
Trebizond Turkey

Trieste Italy
Tripoli Libya
Troisdorf West Germany
Troon UK
Trouville-sur-mer
   France
Tuart Hill Australia
Tucson USA
Tunbridge Wells UK
Turin Italy
Turku Finland

U
Ulan Bator Mongolia
Universal City USA
Upper Basildon UK
Upper Saddle River
   USA
Urbino Italy
Utrecht Netherlands
Uum al-Quaiwain Uum
   al-Quaiwain

V
Vaduz Liechtenstein
Valletta Malta
Vancouver Canada
Varese Italy
Vatican Vatican
Veliko Tirnovo Bulgaria
Venice Italy
Versailles France
Versoix Switzerland
Vevey Switzerland
Vichy France
Vienna Austria

Virum Denmark
Vittel France
Völkungen/Saar West
Germany

W
Walldorf/Hessen West
Germany
Wangarrata Australia
Warley UK
Warsaw Poland
Warwick UK
Washington DC USA
Watford UK
Wellington New Zealand
West Dover USA
Wexford Ireland
Whitefish USA
White Plains USA
Wicklow Ireland
Wienacht Switzerland
Willemstad Netherlands
Antilles

Winchcombe UK
Windsor UK
Wolfsburg West
Germany
Woodstock UK
Worcester USA
Wormley UK
Wroclaw Poland

Y
Yaoundé Cameroun
Yazd Iran
Yeovil UK
Yeungham South Korea
York UK
Yundum Gambia

Z
Zaandam Netherlands
Zomba Malawi
Zurich Switzerland

DIALLING CODES

A nation-by-nation guide to the correct international dialling codes for every country on earth (valid for the UK only).

ABU DHABI
  Abu Dhabi Town
    010 971 2
  Alain   010 971 3
AJMAN
  All places   010 971 6
ALGERIA
  All places   010 213
ANDORRA
  All places   010 33 078
ANGUILLA
  All places
    010 1 809 4972
ANTIGUA
  All places   010 1 809 46
ARGENTINA
  Bahia Blanca
    010 54 91
  Buenos Aires   010 54 1
  Campana   010 54 328
  Cordoba   010 54 51
  La Plata   010 54 21

Mar del Plata
  010 54 23
Rosario   010 54 41
Santa Fé   010 54 42

BAHRAIN
  All places   101 973
BELGIUM
  Aalst   010 32 53
  Antwerp   010 32 31
  Blankenberge
    010 32 50
  Brugge   010 32 50
  Brussels   010 32 2
  Charleroi   010 32 71
  Dixmude   010 32 51
  Doornik   010 32 69
  Ghent   010 32 91
  Kortrijk   010 32 56
  Liège   010 32 41
  Mechelen   010 32 15
  Mons   010 32 65

Namur   **010 32 81**
Oostende   **010 32 59**
Turhout   **010 32 14**
Verviers   **010 32 87**
Zeebrugge   **010 32 50**
BERMUDA
All places   **010 1 809 29**
BRAZIL
Belem PA   **010 55 91**
Belo Horizonte
010 55 31
Brasilia   **010 55 61**
Curatiba   **010 55 412**
Fortaleza   **010 55 85**
Natal   **010 55 84**
Recife   **010 55 81**
Rio de Janeiro
010 55 21
Salvador   **010 55 71**
São Paulo   **010 55 11**
BRITISH VIRGIN ISLANDS
All places   **010 1 809 49**
BRUNEI
Seria/Mumong
010 673 3
Tutong   **010 673 4**

CANADA
Brandon   **010 1 204**
Calgary   **010 1 403**
Corner Brook
010 1 709
Edmonton   **010 1 403**
Gander   **010 1 709**

Halifax   **010 1 902**
Hamilton   **010 1 416**
Kingston   **010 1 613**
London   **010 1 519**
Medicine Hat
010 1 403
Montreal   **010 1 514**
Moose Jaw   **010 1 306**
Niagara Falls
010 1 416
Ottawa   **010 1 613**
Quebec   **010 1 418**
Regina   **010 1 306**
Saskatoon   **010 1 306**
Toronto   **010 1 416**
Vancouver   **010 1 604**
Whitehorse   **010 1 403**
Winnipeg   **010 1 204**
CAYMAN ISLANDS
All places   **010 1 809 94**
COSTA RICA
All places   **010 506**
CUBA
Havana   **010 53**
CYPRUS
Larnaca   **010 357 41**
Limassol   **010 357 51**
Nicosia   **010 357 21**
Paphos   **010 357 61**
CZECHOSLOVAKIA
Bratislava   **010 42 7**
Ceske Budejovice
010 42 38
Plzen   **010 42 19**
Prague   **010 42 2**

DENMARK
Arhus   010 45 6
Copenhagen (Inner)
   010 45 1
Copenhagen (Outer)
   010 45 2
Esbjerg   010 45 5
Helsingor   010 45 2
Odense   010 45 9
Roskilde   010 45 2
Viborg   010 45 6
DOMINICA
All places
   010 1 809 449
DOMINICAN REPUBLIC
All places   010 1 809
DUBAI
Dubai Town
   010 971 4

EL SALVADOR
All places   010 503

FAROE ISLANDS
Torshavn   010 45 42
FIJI
All places   010 679
FINLAND
Espoo   010 358 15
Helsinki   010 358 0
Kuopio   010 358 71
Tampere   010 358 31
Vantaa   010 358 14

FRANCE
Amiens   010 33 22
Avignon   010 33 90
Biarritz   010 33 59
Bordeaux   010 33 56
Boulogne-sur-mer
   010 33 21
Brest   010 33 98
Calais   010 33 21
Cannes   010 33 93
Cherbourg   010 33 33
Clermont-Ferrand
   010 33 73
Corsica   010 33 95
Dieppe   010 33 35
Dijon   010 33 80
Le Havre   010 33 35
Lille   010 33 20
Lyon   010 33 7
Marseille   010 33 91
Montpellier   010 33 67
Nantes   010 33 40
Nice   010 33 93
Paris (City)   010 33 1
Perpignan   010 33 68
Reims   010 33 26
Rouen   010 33 35
St Tropez   010 33 94
Strasbourg   010 33 88
Toulon   010 33 94
Toulouse   010 33 61
Tours   010 33 47
FUJAIRAH
All places   010 971 91

GAMBIA
  Banjul **010 220**
  Brikama **010 220 94**
GERMAN DEMOCRATIC
  REPUBLIC
  Berlin (East) **010 37 2**
  Dresden **010 37 51**
  Leipzig **010 37 41**
  Rostock **010 37 81**
GERMAN FEDERAL
  REPUBLIC
  Aachen **010 49 241**
  Berlin (West)
    010 49 30
  Bonn **010 49 228**
  Bremen **010 49 421**
  Bremerhaven
    010 49 471
  Brunswick **010 49 531**
  Coblenz **010 49 261**
  Cologne **010 49 221**
  Dortmund **010 49 231**
  Duisburg **010 49 203**
  Düsseldorf **010 49 211**
  Essen **010 49 201**
  Frankfurt (Main)
    010 49 611
  Hamburg **010 49 40**
  Hannover **010 49 511**
  Karlsruhe **010 49 721**
  Kiel **010 49 431**
  Lubeck **010 49 451**
  Mannheim **010 49 621**
  Munich **010 49 89**
  Munster **010 49 251**

  Nuremberg **010 49 911**
  Offenbach (Main)
    010 49 611
  Stuttgart **010 49 711**
  Wuppertal **010 49 202**
GIBRALTAR
  All places **010 350**
GREECE
  Alexandroupolis
    010 30 551
  Argos **010 30 751**
  Athens **010 30 1**
  Corfu (City)
    010 30 661
  Delph **010 30 265**
  Heraklion (Crete)
    010 30 81
  Piraeus **010 30 1**
  Rhodes **010 30 241**
  Thessaloniki **010 30 31**
GRENADA
  All places
    010 1 809 444
GUATEMALA
  Guatemala City
    010 502
GUYANA
  George Town
    010 592 02
  Linden **010 592 04**
  New Amsterdam
    010 592 03

HONDURAS
All places **010 504**
HONG KONG
  Hong Kong
    010 852 5
  Kowloon **010 852 3**
  New Territories
    010 852 12
  Outlying Islands
    010 852 5
HUNGARY
  Budapest **010 36 1**
  Debrecen **010 36 52**
  Kaposvar **010 36 82**
  Pecs **010 36 72**
  Zalaegerszeg
    010 36 92

ICELAND
  Reykjavik **010 354 1**
INDIA
  Bombay **010 91 22**
  New Dehli **010 91 11**
IRAN
  Tehran **010 98 21**
IRAQ
  Baghdad **010 964 1**
ISRAEL
  Afula **010 972 65**
  Akko **010 972 4**
  Ashkelon **010 972 51**
  Beer Sheva
    010 972 57
  Benei Berak **010 972 3**
  Givataim **010 972 3**

Hadera **010 972 63**
Haifa **010 972 4**
Herzlia **010 972 3**
Jaffa **010 972 3**
Jericho **010 972 292**
Jerusalem **010 972 2**
Nazareth **010 972 65**
Ramat Gan **010 972 3**
Rehovot **010 972 54**
Tel-Aviv **010 972 3**
ITALY
  Amalfi **010 39 89**
  Bari **010 39 80**
  Bologna **010 39 51**
  Brescia **010 39 30**
  Cagliari **010 39 70**
  Capri **010 39 81**
  Como **010 39 31**
  Florence **010 39 55**
  Genoa **010 39 10**
  La Spezia **010 39 187**
  Livorno **010 39 586**
  Messina **010 39 90**
  Milan **010 39 2**
  Modena **010 39 59**
  Naples **010 39 81**
  Padua **010 39 49**
  Palermo **010 39 91**
  Parma **010 39 521**
  Perugia **010 39 75**
  Pescara **010 39 85**
  Piacenza **010 39 523**
  Pisa **010 39 50**
  Reggio Emilia
    010 39 522

Rimini   **010 39 541**
Rome   **010 39 6**
Salerno   **010 39 89**
Sassari   **010 39 79**
Taranto   **010 39 99**
Torre del Greco
    010 39 81
Treviso   **010 39 422**
Turin   **010 39 11**
Udine   **010 39 432**
Varese   **010 39 66982**
Venice   **010 39 41**
Verona   **010 39 45**

JAMAICA
    All places   **010 1 809**
JAPAN
    Hiroshima   **010 81 822**
    Kobe   **010 81 78**
    Osaka   **010 81 6**
    Tokyo   **010 81 3**
    Yokohama   **010 81 45**

KENYA
    Langata   **010 254 2**
    Mombasa   **010 254 11**
    Nairobi   **010 254 2**
    Nakuru   **010 254 37**
KUWAIT
    All places   **010 965**

LESOTHO
    Maseru   **010 266 1**
LIBYA
    Benghazi   **010 218 61**
    Tripoli   **010 218 21**
    Tripoli Int Airport
        010 218 22
LIECHTENSTEIN
    Vaduz   **010 41 75**
LUXEMBOURG
    All places   **010 352**

MACAO
    All places   **010 853**
MALAWI
    Blantyre   **010 265**
    Makwasa   **010 265 474**
MALAYSIA
    Bintulul (Sarawak)
        010 60 86
    Ipoh   **010 60 5**
    Kota Kinabalu
        010 60 88
    Kuala Lumpur
        010 60 3
    Malacca   **010 60 6**
    Penang   **010 60 4**
    Taiping   **010 60 5**
MALTA
    All places   **010 356**
MEXICO
    Acapulco   **010 52 748**
    Mexico City   **010 52 5**

MONACO
All places   **010 33 93**
MONTSERRAT
All places
   010 1 809 491
MOROCCO
Agadir   **010 210 8**
Casablanca   **010 210**
Rabat   **010 210 7**

NAURU
All places   **010 674**
NETHERLANDS
Alkmaar   **010 31 72**
Amersfoort   **010 31 33**
Amsterdam   **010 31 20**
Apeldorn   **010 31 55**
Arnhem   **010 31 85**
Breda   **010 31 76**
Delft   **010 31 15**
Dordrecht   **010 31 78**
Eindhoven   **010 31 40**
Flushing   **010 31 1184**
Haarlem   **010 31 23**
Hague, The   **010 31 70**
Hook of Holland
   010 31 71
Leiden   **010 31 71**
Nijmegen   **010 31 80**
Rotterdam   **010 31 10**
Tilburg   **010 31 10**
Utrecht   **010 31 30**
Zwolle   **010 31 5200**
NETHERLANDS ANTILLES
Curaçao   **010 599 9**

St Maarten   **010 599 5**
NEW ZEALAND
Auckland   **010 64 9**
Christchurch   **010 64 3**
Dunedin   **010 64 24**
Gore   **010 64 20**
Hamilton   **010 64 71**
Invercargill   **010 64 21**
Napier   **010 64 70**
Nelson   **010 64 54**
New Plymouth
   010 64 67
Palmerston North
   010 64 63
Rotorua   **010 64 73**
Timaru   **010 64 56**
Wanganui   **010 64 64**
Wellington   **010 64 4**
NORWAY
Alesund   **010 47 71**
Bergen   **010 47 5**
Fedje   **010 47 5**
Kristiansand S
   010 47 42
Oslo   **010 47 2**
Sandefjord   **010 47 34**
Sarpsborg   **010 47 31**
Stavanger   **010 47 4**
Tonsberg   **010 47 33**
Trondheim   **010 47 75**

OMAN
All places   **010 968**

PAPUA NEW GUINEA
   All places **010 675**
POLAND
   Krakow **010 48 94**
   Warsaw **010 48 22**
PORTUGAL
   Almada **010 351 19**
   Aveiro **010 351 34**
   Barreiro **010 351 19**
   Estoril **010 351 19**
   Lagos **010 351 82**
   Lisbon **010 351 19**
   Oporto **010 351 29**

QATAR
   All places **010 974**

RAS AL KHAIMAH
   All places **010 971 7**

ST KITTS NEVIS
   All places
     010 1 809 469
ST LUCIA
   All places (4 fig nos)
     010 1 809 455
   All places (5 fig nos)
     010 1 809 45
ST VINCENT AND BEQUIA
   All places **010 1 809 45**
SAN MARINO
   All places **010 39 541**

SAUDI ARABIA
   Jeddah **010 966 2**
   Mecca **010 966 2**
   Medina **010 966 4**
   Riyadh **010 966 1**
SEYCHELLES
   All places **010 248**
SHARJAH
   All places **010 971 6**
SINGAPORE
   All places **010 65**
SOUTH AFRICA
   Alberton **010 27 11**
   Bloemfontein
     010 27 51
   Brakpan **010 27 11**
   Cape Town **010 27 21**
   Durban **010 27 31**
   East London
     010 27 431
   Johannesburg
     010 27 11
   Kimberley **010 27 531**
   Port Elizabeth
     010 27 41
   Pretoria **010 27 12**
SOUTH WEST AFRICA
   Keetmanshoop
     010 264 631
   Okahandja
     010 264 622
   Windhoek **010 264 61**
SPAIN
   Alicante **010 34 65**

Balearics, The
   010 34 71
Barcelona   010 34 3
Benidorm   010 34 65
Bilbao   010 34 4
Granada   010 34 58
Las Palmas   010 34 28
Lloret de Mar
   010 34 72
Madrid   010 34 1
Malaga   010 34 52
Palma (Majorca)
   010 34 71
Santa Cruz (Tenerife)
   010 34 22
Seville   010 34 54
Torremolinos
   010 34 52
Valencia   010 34 6
SRI LANKA
Bandaranaike Int Airpt
   010 94 315
Colombo Central
   010 94 1
Kandy 010 94 8
SWAZILAND
All places 010 268
SWEDEN
Gothenburg 010 46 31
Halmstad 010 46 35
Helsingborg 010 46 42
Karlstad 010 46 55
Kristianstad 010 46 44
Linkoping 010 46 13
Malmö 010 46 40

Stockholm 010 46 8
Sundsvall 010 46 60
Uppsala 010 46 18
SWITZERLAND
Basle 010 41 61
Berne 010 41 31
Fribourg 010 41 37
Geneva 010 41 22
Interlaken 010 41 36
Klosters 010 41 83
Lausanne 010 41 21
Lucerne 010 41 41
Lugano 010 41 91
St Gallen 010 41 71
St Moritz 010 41 82
Winterthur 010 41 52
Zermatt 010 41 28
Zurich 010 41 1

TAIWAN
Taipei 010 886
TANZANIA
Dar-es-Salaam 010 255
TONGA
All places 010 676
TRINIDAD AND TOBAGO
All places 010 1 809
TUNISIA
Tunis 010 216 1
TURKEY
Adana 010 90 711
Ankara 010 90 41
Bursa 010 90 241
Istanbul 010 90 11

Izmir **010 90 2111**
Konya **010 90 331**
TURKS AND CAICOS
All places
010 1 809 946

UMM AL QUAIN
All places **010 971 6**
USA
Alaska **010 1 907**
Albany (NY) **010 1 518**
Atlanta **010 1 404**
Atlantic City (NJ)
010 1 609
Baltimore (Md)
010 1 301
Boston (Mass) **010 1 617**
Buffalo (NY) **010 1 716**
Chicago (Ill) **010 1 312**
Cincinnati (Ohio)
010 1 513
Cleveland (Ohio)
010 1 216
Columbus (Ohio)
010 1 614
Dallas (Tex) **010 1 214**
Denver (Col) **010 1 303**
Detroit (Mich)
010 1 313
Fort Worth (Tex)
010 1 817
Hawaii **010 1 808**
Honolulu (Haw)
010 1 808
Houston (Tex)
010 1 713

Indianapolis (Ind)
010 1 317
Jacksonville (Fla)
010 1 904
Jersey City (NJ)
010 1 201
Los Angeles (Calif)
010 1 213
Miami (Fla) **010 1 305**
New Orleans (La)
010 1 504
New York City (NY)
010 1 212
Philadelphia (Pa)
010 1 215
Pittsburgh (Pa)
010 1 412
Richmond (Va)
010 1 804
Salt Lake City (Utah)
010 1 801
San Francisco (Calif)
010 1 415
Seattle (Wash)
010 1 206
Toledo (Ohio)
010 1 419
Washington DC
010 1 202
USSR
Kiev **010 7 044**
Leningrad **010 7 812**
Minsk **010 7 017**
Moscow **010 7 095**
Tallin **010 7 0142**

VENEZUELA
  Barqisimeto **010 58 51**
  Cabimas **010 58 64**
  Caracas **010 58 2**
  Ciudad Bolívar
    010 58 85
  La Asunción **010 58 95**
  Maracaibo **010 58 61**
  San Cristobal **010 58 76**
  Valencia **010 58 41**

YUGOSLAVIA
  Belgrade **010 38 11**
  Dubrovnik **010 38 50**
  Opatija **010 38 51**
  Skopje **010 38 91**
  Zagreb **010 38 41**

ZAMBIA
  Kitwe **010 260 2**
  Lusaka **010 260 12**
  Ndola **010 260 26**